A
LARGE
HARMONIUM

A
LARGE
HARMONIUM

A NOVEL

SUE SORENSEN

COTEAU BOOKS

Edited by David Carpenter
Designed by Tania Craan
Printed and bound in Canada at Friesens

LIBRARY AND ARCHIVES CANADA CATALOGUING IN PUBLICATION

Sorensen, Sue, 1962-
    A large harmonium : a novel / Sue Sorensen.

ISBN 978-1-55050-460-6

    I. Title.

PS8637.O65L37 2011   C813'.6   C2011-905061-7

10 9 8 7 6 5 4 3 2 1

COTEAU
BOOKS

2517 Victoria Avenue
Regina, Saskatchewan
Canada S4P 0T2
www.coteaubooks.com

AVAILABLE IN CANADA FROM:
Publishers Group Canada
2440 Viking Way
Richmond, British Columbia
Canada V6V 1N2

Coteau Books gratefully acknowledges the financial support of its publishing program by: the Saskatchewan Arts Board, the Canada Council for the Arts, the Government of Canada through the Canada Book Fund, the Government of Saskatchewan through the Creative Economy Entrepreneurial Fund, the Association for the Export of Canadian Books and the City of Regina Arts Commission.

For my largely harmonious family
My sons, Peter and Theo
and Michael, best husband ever.
With love.

Let her fuss for a while if you can stand it.

Benjamin Spock and Michael B. Rothenberg,
Dr. Spock's Baby and Child Care
(1985 edition)

CHAPTERS

YOU CAN NEVER PREDICT

I SAY I WILL BUY THE JIFFY MARKERS MYSELF.

For Kate, the office assistant who sometimes helps me, has her work cut out for her, and none of the students who had volunteered to help with the campus peace crusade have turned up this morning. It's eleven thirty-five and I'm done my morning honours seminar in classic novellas. *Notes from Underground* depresses them all, and I can no longer remember why I put it on the syllabus. It was certainly a mistake to put it last. Classes are done this week, and students are focussed on exam anxiety already. Dostoyevsky is tipping them over the edge, and I feel responsible. My one dependable Student Peace Movement member, Jee-Anne, is coming at twelve thirty to pick up posters to put up around campus. Except they aren't made yet.

At eleven forty-five I find myself on my hands and knees on my office floor, getting high on Jiffy Marker fumes, wondering how many years I will be making posters to stop violence against women, to start drinking fairly traded coffee, to get cracking on raising funds for refugees and generally to pretend to put the kibosh on the screwed-up behaviour that makes the notion of a civilized world so laughable. I'm less into this than I was in the fall. April is tough: I can visualize the towers of exams that will await marking very soon, and am already feeling guilty about the fact that only large amounts of chocolate and caffeine, both frowned upon by the Weight Watchers commandant who runs the weekly meeting in our neighbourhood, will get me through.

I have a nice stack of Bristol-board posters for Jee-Anne and I slow down, taking stock, rather belatedly, of my penwomanship. Jiffywomanship? Hector always says I have a "fine teacher's hand," but he usually says that when he wants me to write a particularly difficult sympathy card or something. Today my heart is not in it, and my lines, announcing the information picket at the consulate tomorrow, slant towards each other in a decidedly unprofessional manner. Whatever. Where is Jee-Anne? Hector is picking me up for lunch at twelve thirty and we have an unvoiced plan to take off, some-where, for the afternoon. I am done teaching for today. It is Friday, the Friday of one of the busiest weeks of term for both of us. At breakfast, before dropping Little Max off at daycare, we consulted our calendars and made the date for lunch. The way Hector said "lunch" made me look at him closely. He raised his eyebrows over Little Max's brown head, shovelling Cheerios into him but looking intently at me the whole while. I met his eyes, large and brown, often partly obscured by a flopping mass of brown hair that will tumble down over his face when he is active or dis-tracted. This morning I saw his eyes clearly, because he accidentally got a short haircut that is causing him a good deal of chagrin.

"You don't have any appointments?" I asked. "It's your office hour on Friday afternoon."

"I'm cancelling it." He looked at me. No smile. The eyebrows were returned to standard placement. I looked back at him, tried to make my face as enigmatic as his. This was hard for me. I have no acting skills.

"What time do we have to p-i-c-k u-p the b-a-b-y?" I spelled all the words that might set off Little Max, who loves his daycare but pretends to get upset at any mention of it. Unless he mentions it, at which point it is okay to discuss it: his favourite daycare workers, the spray-paint-macaroni crafts, the sandbox, the exotic snacks, the fabulous field trips to petting zoos, the waterplay table (what skill does this teach?).

"How about the very latest time possible?" Hector was on his feet, getting the dishcloth to wipe the milk from his good dark green shirt. He fetched a clean baby washcloth from the basket on the wall and wiped up Little Max, who shouted his disapproval. Little Max skittered off into the living room, crashed into his new junior drum kit, kicked a Frisbee and several *I Spy* board books under the couch. The cats, not accustomed yet to the noise of the drum kit, leaped for the stairs and disappeared around the landing.

We put the finishing touches on Little Max's lunch: pudding (vanilla, never anything else on pain of death), little chunks of bread and meat in separate containers (large sandwich-like articles are treated with disdain), a cheese stick (expensive, sometimes hated, sometimes revered by Little Max, impossible to predict which on any particular day), grapes cut precisely in half, crackers. Would it all come back again untouched, attended by an extremely pale three-year-old exhausted from refusing to eat or rest or drink all day because we've had the temerity to go to work at the university and leave him with the daycare workers he adores? The child is baffling. His personality is huge, his will stronger than ours by far.

Hector drew a cat on a Post-it note and wrote the word "Love" in different languages all over it. He slipped it into the lunch kit and zipped it up. "The very latest time possible," he repeated. "How about that?"

There was, apparently, nothing in his voice out of the ordinary, but I stood closer to him, letting the shoulder of my superscary academic power suit touch his shoulder. I bolted my vitamins and looked at the clock. "We don't normally need that long," I said. "But that sounds very good to me."

Now, at noon, he is late, but only by a few minutes, and the student has not yet arrived to collect the posters anyway. I check my email again. I'm looking for a message from the editor of a journal I sent a paper to ages ago, and nothing is happening. I no longer even remember what the paper was really about, but found my research notes in a file folder the previous day and was reminded of the pending nature of this project. I sent them a query. I could use some good news but am doubtful. What did I call it? "Heart (Attack) of Darkness: Myocardial Infarcations and Other Afflictions in High Modernism." Perhaps a mistake. I let my friend Tom in History talk me into that one. We were in the faculty club and it seemed perfect at the time. Well, it's not his career that's being ruined, is it? He's had tenure for years and has already started to wear bedroom slippers to class.

There are only emails with subject lines like "You too can have multiple Orgazzzmmms" and "Be a Backgammon Master!" Is this really a burning need, I wonder? I briefly try to picture all the potential backgammon addicts that this spam will attract, but fail. Is backgammon mastery really up there with the need to gamble, have penis extensions and find deep discount pharmaceuticals? I hesitate at the subject lines "Big Conference" and "Super Milton." They could be legitimate. I open the first one, holding my breath, waiting for some vicious virus to devour my computer. Nothing happens. The message is gibberish. I delete it.

A moment later, Jee-Anne collects the posters and then Hector calls. "I'll be down in a minute," he says. His office in the Music Department is two floors above mine in the English Department. "Think about where you want to go for lunch."

"I thought that was settled." I try to say it in a manner both provocative and neutral, but he is already gone. I could hear the tension in his voice. He doesn't get along with the head of his Department, and there is a leadership review ongoing, in which Hector has taken an unaccustomed stand, bold and assertive. He doesn't want to be head, but I can see that the younger members of the Department are ready to line up behind him if he chooses to stand for the position. He feels responsible for their well-being, but doesn't want to do the administrative work. Something is up.

He is distracted when he arrives at my door, but he doesn't want to talk about the Music Department. When I ask if he is sure he can take the afternoon off, he obliquely reminds me that he is conducting the university choir tonight at the final game of the regular season for the Badgers, Winnipeg's semi-pro hockey club. They will sing "O Canada" before the puck drops, and, at the end of the first period, a short medley of Neil Young and Guess Who songs, in awfully tasty arrangements that Hector has somehow concocted. "Do you want to bring the baby?" he asks. Little Max is not a baby, but somehow speaking of him in this way gives us a peculiar joy. I've never analysed why. Perhaps because we talked about having a baby for so long, and when it finally happened it was such a stunning thing for us that we can't leave the idea alone, even though Little Max is now a toddler.

Thinking of Little Max, now supposedly settling into "rest time" at daycare (but more likely demanding that the workers read T. S. Eliot's "Growltiger's Last Stand" to him over and over again), gives me a twinge of guilt and regret. It always does. Even when he's with me I feel guilty that sometimes he isn't. I almost ask Hector if he doesn't think that maybe we should go pick him up and all go home together early, and then I catch a glimpse of Hector's face at my side as we head down the hall, past the bucket catching the ceiling leak near Biology, towards the parking lot. I clamp my lips together, and we go home.

I OFTEN FEEL LOW IN APRIL, but it has not yet hit this year. I am still in the last week of classes, and although I am tired of teaching and the constant running from appointment to meeting to class, I also find it exhilarating. And meaningful. Most of what I do is still new enough to me that it actually feels like it means something. Hector has been at it longer, and sighs more about Department meetings and committee meetings and Senate meetings and gruesome end-of-year windups that are meant to be fun and end up being, well, gruesome. Later in April, I know, depression is likely to hit, and I need to formulate a plan. Without the structure of classes, without those faces waiting for me in English 100 or The Short Story, I flounder for a while. I have no particular interest in furthering my career or doing something for myself. I like doing things for them, the students. If someone asked me to write a book, I would be galvanized to do it because someone pretended that they needed me to do it. But no one ever asks academics to write books, unless their names are Harold Bloom or Noam Chomsky or Camille Paglia (but is she a real academic, I wonder?). But the rest of us, toiling away in places that are absolutely not Duke or Harvard, or even St. Francis Xavier, don't exactly have publishers and editors beating our doors down with offers to illuminate the world about our thrilling research into "The Saskatchewan Bildungsroman," or "Homoerotic Tropes in Early Dickens."

So I am trying to make a schedule of moderate academic activity to start in May. Still send Little Max to daycare most days, work on the outline of a book, maybe on Iris Murdoch, maybe on Canadian comedy. Get some exercise – walk to the university at least three times a week, or ride my bike, which has not moved from our garage in five years. And I will write more Amnesty International letters. And do more gardening. And teach Little Max to garden. And volunteer at that refugee drop-in centre. And work on that children's manuscript I abandoned in 1987. And so on. Already I am starting to feel the depression. I will do none of this.

But I am not depressed enough that it hampers me this afternoon. Nor does Hector's anxiety about the internecine struggle in the Music Department seem to bother him overly. We do not even bother with food but head up to the bedroom, stepping over already-damaged pieces of the junior drum kit on the stairs.

Hector closes the curtains. "Did you hear about the big grant that Juanita Braun-Epp got, in Sociology?" I shake my head and hold up two jewel-coloured brassieres that are his favourites. I have an old worn beige one on for work and intend to change. He likes to choose, and then he likes to watch me get undressed and dressed, or dressed and undressed. He's not fussy. "She's doing a study of Edwardian sleeping porches in Winnipeg houses and apartment buildings. Their impact on family life. The economic status of those with sleeping porches. I don't know what all." He considers the transparent black brassiere and the deep magenta lacy one. He is a connoisseur of such things and takes his time considering their possible impacts on his afternoon. I like this pace. I can hear the phone ringing on the first floor but we both ignore it. I watch his eyes as he thinks about the black one, the magenta one, weighing their various assets. They have no liabilities, frankly. Even I can see that. It was Hector who introduced me to lingerie, when we first met fifteen years ago, and I am a complete convert now. But he had to school me, and a lovelier course of study I never embarked upon. I used to have a selection of solid colour cotton underpants, sensible and serviceable, and never wore a brassiere if I didn't absolutely have to. His eyes move back and forth from the brassieres to me, standing half undressed by the closet. He is sitting on the bed, which we never bothered making this morning, and he pulls himself back towards the pillows, piling them up behind him, settling into what he sometimes calls his "pasha" mode.

"I don't quite see why that's sociology," I say while his eyes move over me. "But then I've never understood what sociology is, frankly. I'm sure there's something wrong with someone who claims to be an academic and doesn't know what sociology is."

"There's nothing whatsoever wrong with you," says Hector. His voice has become different. His other voice returns briefly and he says, "Yeah. Couldn't it as easily be a Psychology study? Or politics?"

"I don't know," I say. "Let me see your Psychology study."

"Janey," he says. "That's dumb."

"Yes, it is," I say. And then we stop talking.

THE PERFORMANCE OF THE UNIVERSITY CHOIR at the Badgers game is a huge success, with the audience singing along to "American Woman" with special gusto. Hector will later say he is disgruntled by the reaction, because the choir worked all winter on their annual Bach recital and when it was performed last month the response was polite but mild. The Neil Young/Guess Who medley was something he and the choir threw together in a couple of weeks and the crowd can't get enough. Little Max sits on my knee and claps along to "Clap for the Wolfman" but then gets restless. His hand reaches up and then, purposefully or not – I can't tell – his fingernails rake across my cheek. I gasp and jump out of my seat, barely holding on to Max, whose body now stiffens in anticipation of reproof. "Oh, Max, how could you? Don't hurt Mommy." I hiss the words into his ear and manage to hold his body away from mine as he aims a hard kick at my stomach. I have a sudden memory of lying on a hotel bed, pregnant, crooning a loving, sentimental song to Little Max. We knew his sex and had his name picked out: Maximilian Frederick Erlicksen-Des Roches. By the time I was six months pregnant, I had a half-dozen sentimental lullabies made up that I would sing to the baby, and Hector was working on a more complicated composition for him, something based on *The Goldberg Variations*. The composition process did not survive the insanity that arrived the day that Little Max did. Hector never got past variation nine. Twenty-three to go. Twenty-three that will never be written, if my hunch is correct.

What was I doing in a hotel room, singing to a fetus? I try to remember as I swing a backpack, Little Max's coat and rubber boots and Little Max himself up the steep stairs of the hockey arena. Too late, I remember Hector and turn to look down at the ice where the choir has been singing, hoping to be able to catch his eye and motion towards the door. But the choir is already dispersing, and I can only see Hector's brown head moving through the gate in the boards. Little Max has stopped kicking now, and I see one of my first-year students watching me from the back row of this section of seats. I compose my face, trying to erase all traces of anger and shame. It was a wedding, I remember, but I don't remember whose, and we had to travel out of town. Staying in a hotel was and is such a novelty for us, such an exercise in hedonism, that I was loathe to leave the room, and while Hector visited with relatives I stayed on the gigantic king-sized bed as long as possible, singing to a child who, I now think bitterly, was not worthy of any of the sweet sentiments we expended upon him. I think back to our longing for this child and then am recalled to the less sentimental present by

Little Max's current silence. It is a tense and devious silence, I believe. He is plotting something.

He arches his back as I try to buckle him into his car seat, making it impossible to accomplish. I prevent myself from swearing and step back for a moment, breathing deeply and deliberately, trying to will myself into the actions of a loving and responsible parent. "Hey, honey," I say. "Knock knock."

His back relaxes and he automatically responds. "Who's there?" I quickly move in and finishing the buckling, kiss him on the check and step back before he can swing at me again. "Dwayne," I say, climbing into the front seat. I have to prompt him to say, "Dwayne who?" and only a parent could understand his enunciation anyway. "Dwayne the bathtub, I'm dwonding," I say, and start the car. He is new to knock-knock jokes but is fond of them. He does not laugh at this one – who would? – and I wonder if the concept of drowning has even come up yet in his world. Probably not. Does it figure in any Maurice Sendak or Margaret Wise Brown books? No, I don't think so. Although Margaret Wise Brown was one weird dame. Drowning is the least of the mayhem in Roald Dahl stories, but Little Max hasn't encountered Dahl yet. Little Max *is* a Roald Dahl story, I decide.

Things are quiet, and apparently equilibrium is returning to our wounded mother-toddler relationship as we drive home. I briefly wonder about Hector's mode of return, but this sort of thing has happened often since Little Max was born, and both of us are used to it, accustomed to asking colleagues for emergency rides or catching the bus. Once, as a baby, Little Max vomited profusely all over Hector just as we were walking into the keynote address of a conference that both Hector and I were interested in. We had fantasized that the baby would sleep peacefully through it and let us be. What fools we were. Without a word, Hector and Little Max turned, and I entered alone, briefly ashamed at the relief I felt to be on my own. Then I was caught up in the activity of the conference, and only at lunchtime did I realize that my wallet was in the baby's diaper bag and I had to beg money from an acquaintance to get some food. Now we are careful to have a few dollars, our keys and a bus token with us at all times, in case the other is swept away in Little Max's Imperium. I hear Little Max's voice now, and look back at him in the rear-view mirror. It is dark, and I mostly see big brown eyes, like Hector's, but when the street lights sweep over him I also see the mop of brown curls and the mark on his cheek where we have unsuccessfully tried to remove a Wile E. Coyote tattoo.

"Mama," he says.

"Yes, honey."

"Knock knock."

He has begun to make up his own knock-knock jokes. "Who's there?" I ask and can't help smiling at him. I'm never sure if he can see me in the rear-view mirror as well as I can see him.

"Tree."

"Tree who?"

"Tree and a rock and a wolf." Then his throaty laugh, an astonishingly sophisticated laugh for a three-year-old. I can see him throwing his head back, hurling himself into the laughter. He has now a few dozen of these, all of them nonsense. "Knock knock. (Who's there?) Kitten. (Kitten who?) Kitten in a truck."

It is a week later and the depression I had feared is arriving. Classes are done, and I'm marking manfully. I think of it as manly effort, for some reason. I must analyse that sometime, but am incapable of much thought just now. I can manage marking fine, and can manage still to make love with Hector. When that goes, then I know I'm in trouble. That happens rarely, thank God. I am actually marking with more ease and contentment than Hector. He marks papers and composition and harmony exercises noisily, as if every wrong note, wrong answer is a personal affront. I can hear him in the evenings in our basement studio, working through the piles of assignments, roaring out his disapproval when he tries out a few notes of some student composition on his piano down there and then stops, as if he has tasted something rancid. He keeps hurtling up the stairs, looking for me. I look up from my Jane Austen papers by first-year students. I am in the second-floor office, next to Little Max's room. He is supposedly asleep, but I am reluctant to believe this. I am vigilant, listening for rustling noises. In any case, I like to be close to him when he is asleep. It is one of my best working times. I don't feel like a bad mother when he is sleeping a few feet from me, and then I'm liberated into work.

"Janey, oh Janey," Hector breathes dramatically but very quietly. We are both obsessed with letting Little Max sleep.

I smile but shake my head. "Let's run away," says Hector. "Let's go to the stupidest movie we can think of. Isn't there one with Jennifer Aniston and Vin Diesel? That should be stupid enough. Directed by Oliver Stone? With that guy who used to sleep with

Anne Heche?"

I shake my head again. I do not say that there is no one to look after Little Max. I do not say that I long to run away with Hector and that we haven't seen a movie in six months. I look down at the paper I am marking. "Elizabeth Bennett's pride," it reads, "prevents her from licking Mr. Darcy when he first proposed."

I raise my eyes to Hector's. Now he is pretending to smash his head against the door frame. He utters histrionic but almost soundless moans of madness and anguish. And he hasn't even read the latest delicious sentence from the first-year papers. I try to count through the stack of them on the desk using only my eyes. There were forty when I started; my quota for the day, in order to earn a Manhattan or gimlet, is ten. I know I have marked only four.

Somewhere in the pile of papers on the desk there is a phone number. I start searching and come up with it surprisingly quickly. "Renée," I have written. "774-9666." Someone told me about a teenager in our neighbourhood who is a good babysitter, but I have a horror of calling babysitters for some reason I have never been able to fathom. I love babysitters; don't get me wrong. But I hate calling them. I make Hector do it.

We have had bad luck with sitters in the last while. The most recent one, Paula, three weeks ago when we went to the symphony, turned out to be not much taller than Little Max himself. She said she was thirteen, and she certainly seemed to herd him with confidence towards the VCR as we headed out the door. But I doubted she could even lift him. He is already thirty-five pounds and clearly going to be a strapping lad.

When we came home, it turned out she'd been unable to herd him further than the VCR. They were still there, Little Max wide-eyed with nervous exhaustion and delight at being allowed three straight hours of Disney classics. Paula looked slightly chagrined, but not enough in my estimation. She had tried to get him into bed, she claimed, but she thought the screaming would disturb the neighbours and they'd call the police. I am familiar with this feeling.

Before that, there was Mrs. Mapplethorpe, a widow from down the street whose near-deafness made her impervious to Little Max's howls of rage and thwarted world domination. So we were certain that Little Max got more sleep on the evening we hired Mrs. Mapplethorpe. But the idea that she couldn't actually hear very much at all prevented us from calling her again, although some days, when Little Max is especially trying, we care less about such esoteric issues as basic safety. However, Hector said, there is his collection of rare Les Paul guitars and his massive CD and vintage vinyl collection to consider, and he doesn't want them to go up in flames while Mrs. Mapplethorpe reads her *Chatelaine* magazine, oblivious, on the front porch.

By this time, not getting enough reaction out of his audience, Hector has dropped to his knees in the doorway to the office, quietly miming madness. He is pretending to be a mad dog, I think. I have been standing with this scrap of paper in my hand, watching him absently while I think about what time it is and deciding how badly we need to get out of the house. I close the office door, trying not to catch Hector's rabidly swishing hindquarters. I close him in with me and scratch him on top of his head. I dial the number and ask for Renée. "This is Renée," says a male voice.

I am taken aback. Oh, René, I think. "This is Janet Erlicksen," I say. "I live in the next block, and I think you've babysat for our neighbours, the Braun-Epps. We have a three-year-old. Maximilian." While René confirms his identity as the Braun-Epp sitter, I consider Hector, who is now lying on his back, pretending to be dead.

"I know this is short notice, but it is Friday, and I think you're sixteen, right, so you probably don't go to bed too early. I have to take my husband to a clinic for a, for...ummm." I momentarily go blank. For what? "I have to take him for an emergency injection. Vitamin B12. I mean it's not really an emergency, but it would be best if he had it as soon as possible, and I've got no one to stay with our son. He's asleep already, so it will be really easy to listen for him and read downstairs or something. For a couple of hours?" I try to maintain a level, calm tone but suddenly imagine my tone is pleading, pathetic. Hector's eyes are opening, and he is wiping off imaginary foam from around his whiskers. Before I am off the phone with René, Hector has leaped to his feet and is downstairs. He is looking through the paper at the movie listings and at the same time opening a beer for us to share.

"Brilliant, Janey," he says. "What did she sound like?"

"It's a boy. A teenage boy. He sounded very serious. He sounded more grown-up than us. He immediately asked if Little Max had any allergies or needed any special medications or interventions. He used that word – interventions."

"Are you wearing that?" Hector eyes the long shape-less skirt I have been wearing this evening, the T-shirt that reads: "My funny T-shirt is in the wash." He likes me in shorter skirts. He snorts whenever I trip on the long skirts I like to wear. I frequently do trip, when coming down the stairs from our room. Even as I am looking down at my clothes, considering them, and considering the nine thirty-five screening time for the Bollywood movie at the Globe that Hector has been longing to see, there is a knock at the door.

René is already nearly six feet tall, with messy, long fair hair and the thinnest arms and legs I have seen this side of a supermodel. He is wearing a System of a Down T-shirt and carrying a copy of a Hermann Hesse novel. *Siddhartha*. Well, I think, at least it's not Ayn Rand. We show him around and he is the first babysitter we have ever had who actually makes a checklist as we tell him about things. He demands the phone numbers of two emergency contacts and wants to know all of the things that Little Max finds calming to eat or drink should he wake up. What are his favourite songs? Does he like his door open or closed? René's eyes take in everything as we talk, and I imagine they are probing into the corners of the room to see if our electrical out-lets have those little plastic safety covers.

"*Siddhartha*," says Hector, as we make our escape. "You can never predict."

"No, you can never predict," I agree. "Who reads *Siddhartha* any more? What decade is this?" I jump into the car and yelp, "Getaway car!" It is a line from a Steve Martin routine, and often Hector fills in other bits of the monologue, usually out of order. But now he is concentrating, trying to read a map in the dim late evening light. "What are you looking for?"

It turns out he is looking for a movie theatre we have never been to before, because it is the only place showing a probably execrable new Jennifer Lopez movie. "You hate Jennifer Lopez," I say to Hector.

"Ah, but you can never predict," he returns. "I have decided that I don't hate Jennifer Lopez. I just think she is more or less completely devoid of talent. She has compensating charms." I start to remonstrate, but he interrupts. "No, not as lovely as your compensating charms, Janey."

When we get to the theatre we find that the paper was wrong and the movie started a half-hour ago. This does not seem to bother Hector in the least. We buy two milkshakes and spend the next two hours in the parking lot of the shopping centre. It is one of the best evenings we've had in a long time.

IMPATIENS

HECTOR HAS DISAPPEARED AND WE HAVE ALL THESE bloody annuals to put in. He agreed that we would get them, but now that they're here, he's not. He will devote any amount of time to perennials, but his temperament is not attuned to annuals. They are left to me, and I am terrible with them. Or with any kind of plant.

He said he was going to the office to see if his marker had finally turned up with the last batch of overdue assignments to return to his students. Marks should have been submitted over a week ago, and mine are off my desk completely. Most of Hector's work is almost done, but near the end of April he came down with the stomach flu and turned over some of his assignments to a marker he sometimes uses. I don't know why he uses her, year after year. Chantal. She's supposedly a grad student, and supposedly brilliant, but year after year she seems no closer to obtaining her Master's. She drops out of most of her classes after she's done about two-thirds of the work. And done it well, claims Hector, and most of his colleagues in the Music Department will reluctantly agree with him.

Anyway, that was this morning at ten thirty. When he said he was going to pick up the mystery assignments from Chantal. And now it's getting on for three thirty.

At four I will pick up Little Max at daycare and go to a party up the street. It's a birthday party for one of the kids Little Max knows in the neighbourhood, but it has an adult component attached, and because term is over and ostensibly I am free to do such things, I felt compelled to accept the invitation. It is a combination Tupperware party and some sort of educational toy party. The kind of party where everything is three times as much as it costs at Zellers – and maybe at least two times more durable – but the only reason you buy it is embarrassment. That and a sense of obligation. So not only do I have to buy a birthday gift for this kid, but I have to buy something at his mother's party too.

I rise from the flower bed where I have been pulling weeds (the gardening task I am best suited for) and go indoors to change from a dirty black dress to a clean one. I am glad the May weather is not hot yet. Black is my colour, and every year, about mid-June, I am forced to relinquish it and head into pale blue (looks terrible on my skin), light brown (looks terribler) or red (makes me look hungover). I refuse to wear white. How do women manage white shorts and skirts and blouses? I can't. You can always see my underwear through them, and while this may look provocative on some women, with me it doesn't work. I keep sneaking glances at women crossing the street in summer, women at the table next to me at Earl's...how do they do it? Are they wearing no underwear at all? Special invisible underwear? I should consult a lingerie saleswoman, but they are unnerving creatures.

I shouldn't have been gardening at all today, but working on my book proposal. I have heard of an academic book agent who will, for a fee of course, act as broker with potential publishers. I need a short proposal, but it needs to be exemplary. I have had two false starts this month and cannot settle to a subject. This is both my failing and my strength as a professor. I have too many interests. Students like it, and it makes it relatively easy to teach a wide variety of courses. But my suspicion (and surely the suspicion of my Department head) is that none of my knowledge runs deep enough for me to be a scholar whom anyone will ever take seriously. I started a proposal on female characters in Robertson Davies, but discovered, quite by accident, that an academic in British Columbia whom I know slightly has embarked on a similar project. Then I toyed with expanding a conference paper I had once given on bad mothers in children's books. Not stepmothers, mind. Mothers. That mother in *Good Dog, Carl* who leaves the baby alone with the dog and heads out, all dolled up, with her good purse and those purple gloves. Purple gloves! No woman wearing purple gloves is up to anything but moral mayhem. She's very similar to the mother in *The Cat in the Hat,* who also leaves the children alone, also clicking in and out of the house in a natty outfit and high heels. She doesn't go to the dentist. No sir. And in *Goodnight, Moon* where has the mother buggered off to? That intractable little bunny who won't go to sleep has been left in the care of a rather odd old lady sitting in a rocker. Well, not an old lady at all, of course. An old lady bunny. A grandmother bunny? A nearly deaf and incompetent neighbour old lady bunny? A stranger old lady bunny, paid less than minimum wage to look after the brat bunny? No wonder the little rabbit won't go to sleep, even though his room is full of balloons and expensive toy houses and telephones. Telephones! I never had a phone in my room when I was a kid. The bunny is obviously one of those privileged but neglected kids, like the ones in *Harriet the Spy*, who have everything except their parents' attention. That bunny mother is at a cocktail party in the Hamptons – the house looks rustic but in a swish way – making time with Norman Mailer or some photo editor from *Vogue*.

I consider myself in the bedroom mirror. Am I ready to pick up Little Max, and go through the twice-daily gauntlet of daycare workers' judgements of my clothes and demeanour? Hector says I imagine this. They are too busy, too damned tired to judge you, he says. I see that I have inadvertently picked out an outfit with a deep plunging neckline. This is for Hector. Not for picking up kids from daycare or going to sandwich-container parties. I take it off and hurl myself on the bed. Where is Hector? Has he called, and I've missed it? I run downstairs in my underwear, pick up the phone and listen for the little beeps that indicate a message. Nothing. I climb upstairs again and look at the clock. I have time to hurl myself on the bed one more time, and do so.

The mother in the *Little Bear* books is commendable, I have to admit, and I also have to admit that I have attempted to emulate Mother Bear from time to time. Her key contribution to my maternal lexicon is "You can't have that wish, my Little Bear." Because Little Max has heard this from a revered source – a bedtime book – he accepts it better than he would accept my own original but perhaps unwise version of No. "You can't have that wish, my Little Bear" does sound more acceptable than "Will you bloody well stop asking that?" or "No frigging way, my Little

Benito Mussolini." Which is what I secretly want to say, and occasionally do, but muttered low, so the child can't hear it. He probably does. He picks up everything I'm thinking and feeling anyway, and uses it against me. Unlike Hector. Hector never uses anything against me. But neither does he seem to pick up what I'm thinking or feeling. Not lately. I am heading into a tailspin, the one that arrives every spring, and he either does not notice or does not care. Probably both.

Then there's that mother in *I Wish That I Had Duck Feet,* a Dr. Seuss book that people don't realize is a Dr. Seuss book, written under another one of his pseudonyms. I had this book when I was little, and Little Max likes it too. When I look at it now, the book seems completely about sex, completely phallic. I wish I had a whale spout; I wish I had a long, long tail. The most obvious one is the elephant trunk. Yeah, baby. Should this even be sold in children's departments? Why doesn't Focus on the Family do something about *I Wish That I Had Duck Feet?* Where are the moral arbiters of our time when they are really needed? The mother in that book is another piece of work, let me tell you. Her entire being is bound up in being crappy to her son. Get those duck feet off my clean floor! Get that whale spout out of here right this minute! She is all pointing finger, and natty little high heels (again). Slim-fitting early sixties attractive suburban matron's dress, and lipstick that tellingly turns up black in the pictures but is surely meant to represent red. Wicked red. Fire red. The detail that has always stunned me is the little string of pearls, worn when doing housework and other important chores like chewing out kids for being themselves. For coming in the door with wet duck feet! What is she doing with those pearls on, in the middle of the day, while ostensibly vacuuming? As soon as she boots out the boy, she's probably out the back door, into the convertible (wicked red, fire red), away from Scarsdale and off to a wine and cheese, maybe with Truman Capote and the staff of *The New Yorker*. Maybe she'll meet Jose Ferrer. Or Jason Robards.

And then there are pathetic mothers. What about Charlie's useless mother in *Charlie and the Chocolate Factory*? Surely anyone could do better than the cabbage soup they are supposed to survive on every day. And the mother in Maurice Sendak's *Outside Over There*? I hate to touch that book with my critical gaze, and my idiotic critical rampaging abates for a moment. The pictures are lovely, and I can pore over them for ages. But the mother is so limp, so useless. The father is away, and her life has lost its meaning. So the children must figure out how to take care of themselves, which of course is the lesson of many (if not all) fairy tales and even most kids' books today. Fend for yourself. "When Papa was away at sea, and Mama in the arbour." I find myself falling asleep, saying this line over and over to myself, and suddenly jerk awake. I am still only half dressed, and the time is...damn, it's nearly four thirty. I should have picked up Little Max long ago, and be presenting myself at Joy Berg's by now to learn about how to save leftovers more effectively.

As I'm pulling on a sensible but I hope not too dowdy dark T-shirt and a skirt, I hear the door downstairs. I go down and see Hector's startled face looking up at me in the front hallway, under the Frida Kahlo poster. Beside her bright colours, he looks pale and even more wide-eyed than usual. We speak at the same time. I don't know what I say, exactly, but Hector seems to be saying, "I didn't expect..." We both stop and his eyes sweep the area for Little Max. This pains me, and I know it shouldn't. Don't I do the same thing when I come in? Look automatically for the child to be sure he is all right? Don't I long to hear his shout of joy whenever he lays eyes on either of us after we have been away, even for an hour?

I bend to pull on my good sandals, the ones with heels that aren't falling off, and Hector starts talking about the Departmental review that is ongoing in Music. "The visitation team comes *tomorrow,* not May twenty-fifth. That's what we were told. Brunhilde screwed up the dates, or somebody did. And I've been on the phone all day, trying to get enough faculty rounded up so that we look like a damn Music Department, not some farcical parody of a bloody... stupid, bloody..." He stops and I look carefully into his face.

"I didn't know what you were doing," I say. "I thought...Chantal..."

As I say her name, Chantal's hair comes into my mind, more than her face does. She has hair that can only be described as "raven." There is a great mass of it, just as the hair of beautiful but seductive and untrustworthy women is described in books. A great mass of it. Cold but beautiful women who ruin the lives of all they meet.

"Chantal?" Hector sounds puzzled and I try to discover whether it is a carefully assumed puzzlement. "Ah, the lovely Chantal..."

It is what we have always called her, and it possibly slips out of him automatically, but I am in no mood for

25

this today. "I have to go get Little Max," I say quickly. I hear my hard tone. It is harder than I mean it to be, but already I am out the door. I do not hear whether Hector asks me to wait so he can come too.

THE EDUCATIONAL TOY ASPECT of the party is better than the Tupperware. Little Max and the other children are entertained by a hired clown and fed Goldfish crackers and chunks of apple and let loose in the backyard with a hired teenager. It is René. I have not seen him since last month, and I am surprised at how happy I am to see him. I greet him with genuine warmth, while I realize my greetings for my female neighbours have been careful and correct. René has a calm face that does not betray any special knowledge of me. Maybe he did not notice, that night, that my shirt was buttoned up differently when I arrived home at midnight from how it had been when we left. I ask him if he has a summer job, or special plans. He doesn't seem to have much going on. This appals me, as I already think the kid is a genius.

I find myself asking if he would like a regular sitting job with Little Max. Maybe a regular evening every week. I don't know what I (or we – am I still married to Hector? What is going to happen with Chantal?) would do with such an evening, but I suddenly want it. Woodworking? Yoga? And even – I wonder if I should be consulting Hector as I blurt this out – would he like to do two or three solid weeks of child care when our daycare shuts down for summer holidays? We are thinking of renting a cottage to do some writing or something, but can't decide what to do about Little

Max. Maybe René could actually come with us. It would be a big cottage. It would only be an hour out of town, and if he had a car he could drive in and out a few times a week if he wanted to.

I can't believe I am doing this. It is unlike me, for one thing. To make holiday plans and arrange for child care with such apparent ease. For another thing, I have barely discussed this with Hector and don't know if we can afford it. But something tells me I have to put my hooks into René before some other mother realizes what a catch he is.

"I'll think about it," says René. "Last year I worked at Camp Elijah but it wasn't really my thing."

I've been to a retreat at Camp Elijah. I know what he means. "Although," I say, "there's nothing like Corned Beef Hash Day at Camp Elijah. Yum."

René gives me a look that I feel I will get to know very well. It is an enigmatic look, one that someone else might interpret as judgmental but I decide is sensible. He heads back towards the children and separates two older boys, tugging at opposite ends of a huge water gun. He takes it away, gently. I turn my attention to the expensive educational toys, after glancing out the patio doors at Little Max, who is pouring sand over his feet in the sandbox and studiously disregarding the clown. I look over the wooden puzzles and the multilingual books and try to check my recoil at the astonishing prices. I am half-heartedly dressing a wooden doll in a friendly variety of ethnic costume pieces, sneaking glances out at Little Max in the back every fifteen seconds or so, when the Toy Woman descends. She is the dealer, the Uber-Host, or whatever they are called.

"Have you seen these volumetrically correct cups?"

she asks, and her expression is so bright that I almost have to avert my gaze. She begins to demonstrate all that they can do: stack, nest, measure, aid in gaining mathematical erudition. She does not say "erudition," but once she has said "volumetrically," a word I have never heard before and that automatically impresses me, I feel I am her intellectual inferior. I am accustomed to being the best-educated woman at these sorts of functions and it is one of the reasons I rarely attend them. I don't feel superior to these women, not at all. I am embarrassed by my degrees, which seem to flap around my neck, visible on tacky chains made of paper clips. Albatrosses of acumen. Petrels of pretension. I am useless. I can make my way around the OED, but can I make that delicious dip that Joy Berg is serving around so suavely at this very moment? I took a course in Latin once, but can I do origami or organize a successful party for sixteen rugrats?

The dealer is embarking on a painstaking explanation of what the bright primary colours of the volumetrically correct cups, carefully planned to be in particular combinations if the toddler stacks them suitably, will do to the toddler's super-absorbent brain. Something marvellous will be triggered, and the toddler will find various secrets of existence open to him or her. It's rather like the Mozart Effect, I gather. The woman knows more about colour theory than Matisse and Kandinsky combined, and I feel I must buy the twelve plastic wonder cups, even though they are twenty-nine ninety-five and a rebellious inner voice is saying that twelve recycled applesauce and yogourt containers would be just as beloved in the bathtub, the place for which these are surely destined. I also wonder if I want

Little Max to be so enlightened, to soak up so much, to be capable of so much. It seems to me that he knows altogether too much already, and I look out at him once again, where he is alone at the back fence, practising what appears to be one of those Highland dances done over crossed swords. As I fill out the order form, finding myself also ordering an origami kit (thirty-four ninety-five) and a cultures of the world educational board game that Little Max won't be able to use until he is twelve (forty-eight ninety-five), I raise my eyes automatically again to the patio doors and see that René is heading towards Little Max, holding out a plate of cheese and a large colourful paper airplane.

I escape the Toy Woman and hurry over to look at the Tupperware-type stuff, even though we have so many leftover containers that they spill onto my head whenever I open their cupboard, a cupboard that Hector has named "Hell." No matter what we do to try to organize them, they still lose their lids and fall at my feet every morning. The plasticware catalogue's most expensive item, is, of course, an elaborate system that you build into your cupboard to organize said plasticware. It looks like those beautifully aligned frameworks that Californians in movies have for their clothes closets, all the tennis wear arranged here, all the spike heels there. I think particularly of the character Cher in the movie *Clueless,* using a computer program to pick out her school outfits every morning. I wonder how many hidden Jane Austen adaptations there are besides *Clueless* and *Bridget Jones's Diary.* Are there enough to make a book? I am standing there for quite some time, with a corncob holding system in my hand (only nine ninety-five), when I realize that René is beside me, and Little Max is in his arms. Little Max is strangely quiet, and as I reach for him, he puts his head on René's shoulder and nestles in closer to him.

With anyone else I would be wounded by this, but something about this teenage boy makes resentment or jealousy impossible. He speaks quietly and seriously, and his hand smoothes down Little Max's hair. "It's funny, isn't it?" says René. "He doesn't even know me, because when I was at your place in April, he slept the whole time. But he seems to know me somehow." The other kids are all circled around the hired clown, who is making what appears to be a balloon stealth bomber. "He's frightened by the clown, and he has been telling me, quite insistently, that he would prefer to go home. I think he's really tired." Little Max lifts his head at this and turns to me, nodding. He keeps a grip on René's shoulder.

"Okay," I say, trying not to sound too relieved to be liberated from the party. Little Max is transferred to my grasp at last, with some reluctance it seems.

"Come home too," he says to René. "See Jeremiah."

Most people would look to me for an explanation of this, but René looks to the three-year-old. "I would like to come. Who is Jeremiah?"

Little Max's communication skills dry up suddenly, in the way of toddlers. I try not to speak for him too much, so René and I wait. My son is searching for the right term, I know. He likes to be accurate. "Giraffe?" he finally offers.

"An anteater," I explain. "It's his favourite. Stuffed toy, I mean." I turn to Little Max. "Should we go home? See if Dad would like to order pizza with us?" I look quizzically at René. I'm not sure if he is done here or not, with the birthday party.

"I'm done here," he answers, without my having asked. I can't believe this is the second time I've met the kid. He feels like a younger, more capable version of myself, thinner of course. He is pulling on a jean jacket and going to say goodbye to Joy.

Most of the items I have ordered will be delivered later, but I do leave with the corncob holding system. Joy presents me with two bonus gifts for being the guest who ordered the most junk. Not that she terms it thus. "Janey, in appreciation for your generous order, please accept not only this salad spinner but also this – the very latest in kitchen timers. If you press this button, you choose the rooster chime. If you press this button, you hear a butler's voice calling, 'Madam! Madam!'" She smiles at me. She is pleased with me.

The salad spinner is enormous and orange. Never has anyone made a salad this big. We make our escape, walking the block to our house, René and Little Max discussing superheroes. Who is better, a superhero without a mask, or one with a mask? René responds to all of Max's comments seriously, considering them carefully, answering honestly and fully. We walk in to the smell of a stir-fry. Hector is finishing cutting up the vegetables. At the sight of him I am suddenly overcome with the need to weep, and am confused by my own move of bringing a stranger into our midst. I make vague gesturing movements between the three of them, standing in the kitchen, and then bolt out the back door. I hurl myself to my knees, disregarding my clean skirt, pulling on my gardening gloves. Picking up the trowel, I start digging a hole, and shove in some impatiens. I muse on the name, even as I cry. Why am I crying? Why do I like to plant impatiens?

I both hope that Hector will come out to me, and dread it. He does not come. Through the kitchen window, I can hear René and Hector and Little Max fall into an easy conversation, with lots of laughter, and then I hear them put on an album and start to set the table. Thelonious Monk arrives in the backyard, and I find it impossible to be sad or worried any more. Monk's crazed chords land beside my impatiens. I imagine the notes surging under the blooms, pushing them this way and that, encouraging them somehow to be...to be what? To be patiens?

I am sitting back on my heels, unladylike, doing nothing, when Hector appears at the back screen door. "Coming?" he asks. His voice is normal. He thinks nothing is wrong. He never thinks anything is wrong. I am momentarily enraged, and then the rage dissipates because I don't know what it is about. "Since René is here," Hector says, *sotto voce,* "can we ask him to sit?" I am visited with a rush of happiness, until I hear what Hector says next. "There's that modern dance thing at the art gallery."

I know who is in the modern dance thing. Chantal.

IN MY QUEST FOR A SUITABLE summer research project, I come across some poems I wrote in grad school. They immediately evoke grad school for me, and I spend some time considering what that feeling represents or is worth. Could they be turned into something?

Jacques Derrida Takes the Chicken Out for
Supper

What does it mean? Can it be contained
in any system (oh, sorry, not system)
or belief (oh, sorry, not belief)
of yours (not yours?)?

Can you bracket the fan I hear from another
*   apartment than mine?*
Does slippage include the chicken taken from
*   the freezer for our supper?*

Is your supper like ours? Do you wake
dreading headaches? Do you
delight in small children using big words
*   and in the*
accuracy of their observations and
*   conclusions?*

When you go for walks, does a tree
exist? Or has the word created
the tree?

I'm sorry to be such a bitch (no, not bitch) but
*   I wonder about trees.*
Do you?
For me a tree is always the test, the proof.
It hasn't failed me yet. I don't know
*   why.*
I cannot theorize or explain or refute a tree.

If you came over for a chicken dinner tonight,
*   would we enjoy ourselves?*

> *When I go for walks, sometimes trees are*
> *obscured for me, but not by words.*
> *Words are less powerful than the*
> *oppression of spirit ladled over*
> *everything*
> *by men like you (not you?).*
> *Well, perhaps not spirit, but my spirit.*
>
> *What does it mean? This chicken, this*
> *paralysis, this love, this tree.*

No one has ever read this, although I was beginning to go out with Hector when I wrote it, and it now reads like a love poem to him. Was it meant to be a love poem? I can no longer remember. He only really appears in the last line, although I can suddenly recall that chicken dinner, which was not much of a success, except that Hector and I spent the next three hours in bed. As I recall, one of the most intense encounters in our nascent relationship, and when I got up the next morning, there were the chicken bones still on the kitchen table where we had left them.

I cannot see why I have made the line breaks where I have made them, and I don't know if the poem has any meaning for anyone but me. But I do know that the composition of it occasioned a real feeling of liberation for me that lasted for several days, and helped me not to quit a particularly difficult seminar I was enrolled in. I did not do well, but I did not quit either. In the poem I named, successfully enough, the disquieting feeling of failure and mutiny that I had then, and I could go ahead with grad school, its petty ego squabbles, its unpleasant competitiveness.

I decide that the poem should stay where it is, in a personal archive. It helped me then, but it can't help me now. I need to come up with a new project, and I need to stop worrying about Hector. We went to the modern dance thing, and Chantal wasn't even dancing. She was working backstage, and I saw her raven hair only briefly at the end, as she hauled big duffle bags of costumes out to a van. Hector was quiet all evening, and when he did speak, he would be in the middle of a complicated and anxious thought about his Department review. "If only Gerard Thibideau had finished his dissertation before this," he would say, and then lapse back into silence.

Today, I am waiting in the courtyard of the university, a pile of psychoanalytical books about children's literature on the bench beside me. Hector is supposed to pick me up and we will go home together, after we pick up Little Max. He is late. Then I remember the visit from the external reviewer, and know that Hector will have a dinner meeting with senior music professors and the examining team. He didn't tell me this, as our morning was a flurry. But I know how these things work, so I pick up my books and get ready to head over to the daycare. I remember once, in the first year I knew Hector, waiting for him at the University of Toronto on a day such as this. We were going to have hot dogs in front of Robarts Library, and Hector was unaccountably late. But I was hesitant to leave, and then a music student I knew slightly appeared in front of me, holding out a note.

"Janey: Can you forgive my tardiness? I hope so. Today is the fellowship deadline and I have to get an application in before 4:30 and I have six hundred pages of tedium to fill out. I am sorry. Will you let me take your clothes off sometime around 9:30 this evening? Your place? Your Hector." I remember looking up hastily at the guy who had delivered the note, to see if he had read it or if he noticed my flushed face. Thinking about this note, all those years ago, I feel a flush of warmth again.

And then it is happening again. I feel the skin on my arms prickling, and hear myself gasp a little. A student is standing in front of me, one of Hector's Composition students who also works in the library this spring and summer. He is holding out a note. It looks the same as the one fourteen years ago. I can't recall that Hector and I have discussed this long-ago note recently. How is it possible that this is happening again? Have I summoned this with my memory?

"Janey: Can you forgive my tardiness? I love you. Hey, did I remember to tell you about the dinner with the eastern wigwags?" This is what Hector calls bigwigs. "I will be home by nine, I hope, and will remove every stitch of your clothing. Make sure that kid is asleep. Your Hector." Sometimes Hector and I talk about telepathy. We don't believe in it, but things keep happening that we cannot explain. I stand still, in a patch of suddenly very warm sunlight, and close my eyes. I think hard, towards him. I think things there are no words for. I think, "Forgive me." I think. I send the warmth of this sunlight towards him, up into the building above me. I think. I smile.

JAMNESS

I AM WALKING DOWN THE HALLWAY OF THE ENGLISH
Department as quietly and quickly as possible, hoping
to get into my office and shut the door before Beatrice
Haight sees me. She is two doors down, and usually
her door is ajar. No matter what time of day I am there,
Beatrice is always there first, editing a massive and
apparently important collection of essays about
Coleridge. And an anthology of twentieth-century Irish
poetry for Oxford. And organizing a conference on
twenty-first-century notions of decadence. I'm afraid
that the first time I heard about this conference I
laughed in front of Beatrice, and have regretted it ever
since. She is one of the grimmest women I have ever
met. Always dressed in grey. Always in a suit, even in
this academic downtime. The idea that Beatrice is
acquainted at all with depravity, even in abstract form,
is one of the funniest things I have encountered. Even
though I know that no really dissolute behaviour will
be in evidence at this decadence conference, and it will
all be highly theoretical, I have been unable to keep a
straight face in any of the Department meetings where
it has been mentioned. Hector and I have spent several
amazing evenings planning, over cosmopolitans, guerrilla theatre productions that we could catapult into the
conference proceedings. My favourite so far is that we
will perform scenes from Oscar Wilde's *Salome* while
completely encased in snowmobile gear – helmets, big

37

boots, full snowsuits, those impossible mitts – while a third person, our friend Tom, will interrupt with excerpts from Foucault's *Discipline and Punish* in a cheesy French accent. Hector's favourite idea involves a large harmonium that is gathering dust in a Music Department practice room on the top floor of our university building. He wants me to write an erotic poem where all the key words about naughty bits are replaced with the word *harmonium,* which he will read with dry academic rigour. And Tom, who is tall and ungainly, will try to push the harmonium around the room on wheels or some sort of dolly. I cannot quite envision it. But it sent Tom and Hector into paroxysms when we had Tom over for Chinese food this week, and now Tom is trying actually to write the poem, making emphatic use not only of the word *harmonium* but also, repeatedly, the name *Martha Nussbaum,* a scholar key to his own History dissertation years ago. Tom has a way of saying *Martha Nussbaum* that can send Hector into fits of hiccups.

Maybe it's something about Tom's combined baldness and the way he says *Martha Nussbaum.* Tom matches the stereotype of professorial appearance to some extent: he is tall and bald and serious looking and has a closetful of plaid woollen vests that always clash a little with his corduroy pants. But he has a crooked, wicked smile that throws that impression into disarray. Or at least it does in the faculty club or our living room.

Beatrice hears me fitting the key in my office lock. Her neat grey head immediately pops around the corner of her door. Her hair is always the same, like Margaret Thatcher's or a TV anchorwoman's. Not nice, not ugly, just the same. "Janet, there is someone here I would like you to meet, dear. Do you have a moment?"

I want to say no. But I have lots of moments. I am not working very hard at anything. Today is the day I have sworn I will decide on my research project once and for all. Iris Murdoch? A feminist study of Douglas Coupland? I have been staring at the wall for too long. I have to decide. Or maybe I should start my own journal. Online, of course; no one has time for paper any more. Except how do you read electronic journal articles in the tub, which is where I do lots of my reading? Damn. An electronic journal. Of course. It will make me famous. It will put me on the map. I realize I am standing in the hallway, staring over Beatrice Haight's ear at a hole a student has punched in the wall on the last day of classes. No one has fixed it yet. I have two simultaneous questions: Have I answered Beatrice? I can't remember. And is the zipper on my skirt undone? It feels strange, and yet I can't check it.

"Of course," I say, and head into her office.

"Janet Erlicksen, this is Blanche Grimm. Blanche, Dr. Erlicksen is our Contemporary Literature specialist, and she also teaches in the area of Victorian Studies. Janet, the university has hired Blanche on a one-year contract, with the possibility of renewal, to teach two sections of Introduction to Women's Studies. It is a cross-disciplinary appointment between our Department and Women's Studies. She will teach Gender Anxiety and Emancipation for our Department. I wanted you to meet her since I think you have research interests in common." Beatrice always talks like this. She never takes verbal shortcuts, she never uses contractions and she is always sure to call me Dr. Erlicksen in front of people without doctorates. This is meant to reflect glory on her, I believe, not me. She looks so respectful and collegial. But I imagine I hear disbelief in her voice when she mentions my title. Was there a mistake when I was granted a doctorate? Did I get it from one of those institutions that advertise on matchbooks? When I see people speaking to Beatrice, sometimes I expect to see them tugging their forelocks. Has anyone ever called her "Ma'am"? She turns again, formally, to Blanche. "Dr. Erlicksen is also working on Iris Murdoch."

Not any more. Damn damn damn. I need a clear field. I guess it's Douglas Coupland or a new journal. But what do I know about starting an online journal? I get confused when people talk about C:drives and H:drives on my computer. H? Where is H? I look at Blanche and try to keep from sighing. She is beautiful and raven haired. What the hell is going on around this place? Where are the mousy young women who will let me sleep in peace? When can I stop worrying about my handsome, sexy, Byronic husband?

"Good to meet you, Blanche," I say, and hold out my hand. I see, as I do this, that there is peanut butter smeared all over the space between my thumb and index finger, and I pull my hand out of the handshake hurriedly. Blanche looks at me strangely. I think she is one of those women who always has lipstick on, no matter what. She probably has lipstick on in the shower, buys some special waterproof kind that enables you to swim and drink beer and indulge in heavy French kissing and still have perfect lipstick. And she doesn't look garish or overly made up. Indeed her eyes are hardly made up at all, not that they need it. She has huge dark

eyes, distinguished by a disarming and (I decide immediately) completely false warmth. She looks like a
movie star. In forties movies in particular, women used
to wake up with their lipstick and hair completely in
place. That's the sort of impression Blanche makes.
Women's Studies, my Aunt Fanny, I think. How confused the students are going to be when you start
talking about The Beauty Myth.

The peanut butter is from Max's sandwich. He
wanted a sandwich for breakfast and I had to make it
at the last minute, when I'd already cooked him por-
ridge and scrambled eggs. I want him to eat and keep
trying whatever he asks for. I know this is a mistake.
He never eats much of it. But when he asked for peanut
butter, I had some sympathy. He's not allowed to have
peanuts at daycare, of course, and if I were a kid, I
would find this a hardship. But because it was the third
breakfast I had made for him, it was done in a hurry.
"Welcome," I say, and smile. I am conscious suddenly
of my appearance. An old denim skirt and a discarded
opera T-shirt of Hector's that I have cut the sleeves off
to make a kind of tank top. It is hot in my office in the
summer. The T-shirt is from some production of
Wagner's *Siegfried*. It has a picture of Siegfried finding
the sleeping Brunhilde on a rock, and underneath the
picture is Siegfried's line: "Das ist kein mann!"

This is no man! It occurs to me that this T-shirt will
be a test of whether this Women's Studies prof will be
any fun to work with or not. I search her beautiful face
as her eyes flick over my chest (also not as beautiful as
hers). Her expression is hard to interpret. Will she
smile? I don't think so. Is she disapproving? I can't tell.
Then Beatrice is speaking.

"Janet, dear, I thought it would be very pleasant if you could take Blanche to the faculty club for luncheon today. Could you show her around?" Of course I am unable to say no. I had hoped to eat lunch at my desk and go home early today, hopefully with Hector, if I can find him. This is typical of Beatrice.

I finally escape to my office and close the door, which contravenes the unspoken Departmental policy that our doors should always be open, in case some student wants to discuss the advantages of the three-year versus the four-year BA at a moment's notice. Of course, come on in! Let's look over your academic record. Do you have your science requirement? Have you considered Astronomy...? Oh, you're interested in Anatomy. I don't know much about that... I pull my blinds shut too, and open the drawers of my desk, looking for emergency clothing. Sometimes I have sweaters in here, or extra socks. Today I am looking for a plain T-shirt at least, to wear to the faculty club. I find a green cardigan with a zipper, which makes me look sort of like a female Mr. Rogers. It will do.

I check my phone messages. Hector left the house at eight this morning to work on a response to the initial report of the external review of the Music Department. The real report is not done yet, and after their visit last month the review team sent a letter with a number of questions that needed answering, some of them quite unpleasant. It has fallen to Hector to come up with the tactful responses that he hopes will get them a positive final report. Hector is one of the best writers in a Department not known for its verbal skills. I forgot to discuss supper plans with him, and I hope he's called. He has.

"Janey. It's nine thirty. Where the hell are you? Are you having an affair with our letter carrier, that saucy lad with the spiky hair, three different shades of unnatural yellow? He has a nice bum, don't you think? Call me when you get in. I have exciting news. Jam just called. Jam! He's in town! Isn't that great? Call me."

I feel a little chilly and pull on the cardigan. Jam. Short for James, but no one who knows him well ever thinks of him as anything but Jam. Jam is always in a jam. Jam has a personality that seems very appealing and sort of sweet at the beginning, but sooner or later gets all over everything and makes a big mess. Jam is Hector's best friend from the time he was fourteen when they met at orchestra camp. Jam plays the French horn and wanders around Canada, playing with various brass quartets and doing workshops in schools. He has no ambition to own a house or have a steady job, and boasts that he has slept with women from all ten provinces. He still has to work on the territories. Although Jam is our age, almost forty-two, he looks about twenty and can pack away three martinis or half a bottle of Scotch in an evening and suffer no after-effects. When he's in town, Hector tries to keep up with him but I can't do it any more.

I sit down at my desk and open the last document I worked on, last Friday, hoping it will help me think about what to work on next. It's another poem. It is called "Who is Julia Kristeva and why is she saying these terrible things about me?" I wrote it to entertain Hector, but forgot to show it to him.

I lined up six apples, flayed
on the cutting board the other day

– a day not other enough for my liking –
and wondered whose they were
and cut them
and made them into something else
for the two I love.

I am less anxious than I used to be
about my inability
to understand a damn word the
lot of you are saying.

I made apple crisp.
I saw the snow and the sky.
I looked forward to my boy and my love
coming home.

It is June; there is no snow. But I felt wintry, in a
good way, as I wrote it. Now I turn away from the document and try to think about Jam, what to do with
him, what we should feed him this evening. Jam always
assumes that one can dine out, not being one to think
about the responsibilities of parenthood. Of course
now we have the valuable René, who has become indis-
pensable as a third parent in a matter of weeks. But I
happen to know that René is at a zoology camp for a
week, and so we have to entertain Jam at home,
encouraging him not to laugh too damn loud while we
get Little Max to sleep. Good luck. The man's roister-
ous laugh is legendary.

I try not to recall the time we took Jam to a
Christmas party at our university president's house. I
was new on faculty and anxious about making a good
impression. Jam told the president's husband a long

and very off-colour story about Vladimir Horowitz and a hemorrhoid operation. I am still smarting a bit. Or more than a bit.

I sit and read the letters to the editor in *PMLA* and the *TLS* for a while, thinking there is no point in getting going on anything now that I have to take the fabulous Blanche to lunch. I am trying to remember a single thing she said, and all I can recall is her glossy head of hair and her lipstick. Did she speak? Poor thing. Beatrice never gave her a chance, and I was obsessing over my peanut butter spill and my low-flying zipper. I shake my head in wonder at the care my fellow academics take in their letters to *PMLA*. Each letter is crafted as carefully, argued as brilliantly, as a grant proposal. Or such is the aim. It's only a letter! Why are these people so passionate about the academy, about the state of cultural literacy, about freedom to teach politically volatile topics? I try to remember if I was ever so excited about my responsibilities as a professor as these letter writers seem to be. Do they list letters to *PMLA* on their activity reports at the end of the year, tally them up for tenure review? Now the letters to the *TLS* seem more comprehensible to me. These Brits are as mad as late-July wasps, arguing endlessly about whether one can state with certainty whether Thomas Hardy's wife had syphilis, whether it affects readings of the late poems. People write in saying that their great-uncles met Hardy once, muttering over the state of an uneven cobblestone street in a cathedral town, and stating that he seemed drunk, but now they believe (in the light of the latest evidence) that surely he was venereally unhinged. The letter writers in the *TLS* engage in endless disputes that make the argument over the colour of Emma Bovary's eyes, the feud that Julian Barnes parodies in his novel *Flaubert's Parrot,* seem positively sensible.

I look up and there is Blanche in my doorway. She has knocked. I have not heard, and she pushed open the door. I have lost track of time and she has sought me out for her faculty club chow down. I realize she is looking with interest at my computer screen, and there, displayed in a large font because I had been happily contemplating the thought, is the last line of my Julia Kristeva poem: *I looked forward to my boy and my love coming home.* She looks at me, smiles and says, "Nice." I decide that I like her, and she would be perfect for Jam.

I HAVE TRIED TO FIX WOMEN UP with Jam before, as has Hector, but the results have been uneven. Although I have tried less often and less vigorously than Hector, I like to think that my choices have had more promise. He went out with Kate, the English Department assistant, for two weeks once while he was in Winnipeg, and for Jam this is a long-term commitment. She was enchanted with him – Jam is good-looking, and rather devilish, and Kate, who is in her late twenties and had just finished a long relationship with a flabby North Kildonan accountant, was in the right frame of mind for Jamness. Jam liked her wit and her refreshing pragmatism. He knows a lot of musicians and calls a lot of the flighty female ones "Ariel," appended to their instrument – "Tuba-Ariel," "Flute-Ariel," and so forth. He rightly realized, and was grateful, that Kate was not an Ariel. Kate talked about books – John Updike, Martin Amis, Alice Munro – and Jam, who reads more than one might suspect, was quite taken with this. I don't know what happened in the end. I do know that Kate is interested in having children, but surely she didn't get into that so soon. If she did, no wonder Jam took off. Hector's best contender over the years was a long-weekend attachment that Jam formed with a wait-ress named Margie in New York City. Hector and Jam were at a jazz festival there, a long time ago, and although Margie was already in her forties and the boys at the time were in their twenties, she worked in an exotic location (the Oyster Bar in Grand Central Station) and Hector knew that Jam would like this and set them up. But it turned out that Margie spent all her spare time trolling flea markets and head shops, looking for Iggy Pop and Velvet Underground paraphernalia, and even for Jam this seemed less than imposing for a life's work. "Imagine," he said later, "being called to account on the Last Day. What do you have to say for yourself, Margie from the Oyster Bar? Well, I have amassed the largest collection of Lou Reed t-shirts on the eastern seaboard, St. Peter. And look at this great Stooges night light! Only one hundred and forty were ever manufactured." Jam snorted, not the way that other people snort, briefly, but long and repetitively. It is rather charming.

I am on the way home on the number eleven bus, with Little Max, because Hector and Jam are still en route from the airport. Jam's French horn apparently has been lost by Air Canada. I wonder why he checked it; he usually does not. Little Max is sitting quietly beside me, watching for cement trucks. He counts them, and presents the number, usually wildly inaccurate, to Hector as a present. To the best of my knowledge, he has seen none today, but claims to have seen seven.

He is either tired or thoughtful. Or maybe plotting something. I am thinking of my lunch with Blanche, who is rather mysterious and no less beautiful now that I've seen her eat a Reuben. We had a good time; she said she coveted my "Das ist kein mann!" T-shirt, which immediately won me over. But she has such a privileged background that I can't help but be suspicious of her. Both her mother and her father have distinguished careers in the Psychology faculty at the University of Toronto, and Blanche is coming off a big postgraduate fellowship, a Killam. I become defensive, thinking of my massive student loans and my tiny IODE and CUPE scholarships, won more because of weird family connections and esoteric qualifications than any cleverness in me. ("Available to married youngest daughters whose fathers were veterans of the Korean conflict and whose mothers led 4-H groups during the years 1974-1982, and whose older siblings are all members of trade unions.") I have never been sure what postgraduate fellowships are, what they mean, what they are meant to accomplish. I never even applied for them, because I couldn't figure them out, and was too embarrassed to ask by that point. It's like the term *festscrift*. What is that exactly? Why are they done? And the category *belles lettres*? Hector looks at me and grins when I ask him about such things. "Oh, Janey, as if," he says. "You know exactly what that means."

Little Max begins to drum his Little Mermaid running shoe against my leg, rubbing dirt and grass all
over my shin. We are getting close to home, and I
reach up and pull the cord. Mistake. He wanted to
do this. He starts to yell, and hurls his Bugs Bunny
lunch kit down the aisle of the bus. I scramble to get
it, and no one moves to help me. The kid is getting
louder, and the bus has been at our stop, the doors
open, for a bit now, and Max and I are a long way
from the door. I pick him up, trying to face him away
from me so that his teeth and nails and kicking feet
can do the least damage. To me anyway. But I worry
for my fellow passengers and pick my way with care
through the crowded bus. The passengers are silent,
listening to Max. "You are wicked!" he shouts.
"Never do that again!"

We emerge on the hot pavement, Max yelling and
spinning, his feet and arms, surprisingly strong, swinging at me. I stand there, submitting to him. It is not
even an effort today to keep my temper. There is no
temper to keep. There is no anger in me, just acres of
sadness that open in front of me in an alarmingly familiar way. Oh God. I suddenly feel so tired, so worn and
worthless that I could lie down here on the sidewalk in
front of the Dairy Queen and stay until someone
scraped me up and dumped me somewhere. I don't care
where. My day suddenly rewinds before me, in all its
futility. My weak-hearted attempts to put on interesting
clothes this morning. My stupid gaping mouth as I let
Beatrice Haight's agenda wash over me once again.
How lank and mousy my hair must have looked next
to Blanche's at lunch. And most of all the fact that this,
this was the day that I was finally going to decide on

my research project and get moving on it. And what had I done? Read in a desultory way, fiddled and deleted. Done nothing. And as a mother, well, the failure is in evidence before me, the shrieking, hitting child whose red face I can hardly recognize.

A large harmonium. The phrase comes at me again, and, as Little Max stops yelling and I stand there, I can hear its ramifications. It sounds like harmony and then some, harmony with all the stops pulled out. Hector has played a harmonium for me. It is a ridiculous instrument but makes a fabulous noise. I do not hear so much the lascivious possibilities that Hector and Tom hear in the word, but I do hear a call to what my life with Hector and Max should be. Could be. But why isn't it? Little Max hurtles himself towards me now, with some need I cannot understand, and buries his head in my skirt, bunching up the fabric in his little fists. I pick him up.

COCKTAIL HOUR

I AWAKE THIS MORNING OUT OF A PROFOUNDLY WEIRD sleep in which I have had a series of short, intense, lively, swirling dreams involving minding children, drawing maps, eating cake, drinking coffee, avoiding angry women and seducing faceless men. I hear Little Max shouting from his room. "Where is everybody?" he yells, and I wonder how long he has been yelling this. Where *is* everybody?

I know instantly, although I am turned the other way, that Hector is not in bed beside me, although it is only seven thirty on a Saturday morning, and he is not normally an early riser. My heart pounding as it always does when Little Max calls for me, I stumble towards his room, desperately needing coffee after the cocktails with Jam last night. Far too many cocktails. Jam here means more drinking. Not good for me. Not good particularly for me.

But Jam staying with us has been going surprisingly okay. I have to admit that I have a big soft spot for him just now because he is going to make it possible to rent the cottage out near Grand Beach that Hector and I thought we couldn't afford. He'll share the cost, and we go on Monday. And Little Max loves Jam, who is very good with him. They read great piles of library books in the hot afternoons, and I like sitting nearby with an iced coffee, listening to them. Jam likes the same old picture books that I do, and finds in them similarly ribald elements that he relishes. Take *Woody and Snowy,* an admittedly obscure one that delights all of us, although for different reasons. Max listens intently to the overt moral about friends helping out friends, although I'm sure he has no plan to try this out in real life. Jam and I are agog over the plot, which involves two bears, one brown and one white, lying down on top of each other in different terrains to prevent enemies from spotting them. Or *Pretzel,* with its astonishingly candid insistence on a dog's obsession with how long he is. Well, yes, he is a dachshund. But still.

Little Max and I head downstairs, and I am even more appalled than usual, because of my slight hangover, by the state of the front hall. Toy teacups, rubber boots, empty yogourt containers. At least I hope they're empty. Stuffed dogs, bears, moose, otters and even a lobster. Our young cat, Adele, is sleeping on a sweatshirt of Jam's that lies near the couch. It is a pink Fleetwood Mac shirt that Jam wears with flair, just to prove he can. He hates Fleetwood Mac, and the colour looks hideous. But he has still picked up women while wearing it, although (even he admits) not top-drawer women. Helen, the older, fatter cat, has disappeared into the basement. It threatens to be a hot day, and she likes it down there. Did we really not pick up any of this mess yesterday? Normally I would make a pass, however half-hearted, through the main rooms as I head up to bed.

I brew some coffee, surprised that there is none made already if Hector and Jam are up, and find that Little Max is, amazingly, eager to eat a banana cut up on his corn flakes. The Hide-A-Bed in the living room is already folded up. Where are they?

I am trying to do a little yoga in the kitchen when they turn up. I am getting a headache, and sometimes yoga helps keep such things at bay. Little Max is briefly occupied at his easel in the back room, so I make it through some vague initial stretches and a few variations of Proud Warrior before he attacks, unfortunately when I am at my most vulnerable, in the Downward Facing Dog pose. I yelp and tumble to the floor. "Oh, Max," I hear myself say. "Don't hurt Mommy." What a stupid thing to say. If someone said that to me, I would want to smack into her again. Downward Facing Dog had been feeling really good too, with all the blood moving in strange and unaccustomed paths all over my body. But now I am too nervous to stick my butt up in the air like that again. Once, when he was just crawling, Max chomped me on an exposed thigh while I was doing Happy Baby, an admittedly ridiculous but very relaxing pose that involves lying on your back and waving your legs in the air above you.

I give up on the yoga, and none too soon, as Hector and Jam are coming in the back door, and my nightgown has been sliding all over the place, particularly during Downward Facing Dog. Little Max rushes for them, beaming. Looking angelic. Naturally. The two men are looking disgustingly fit and healthy, which shouldn't be possible. They have been running along the Assiniboine before it gets too hot. Hector does not usually run, but he's allowed Jam to talk him into taking it up again. They don't even want coffee, but just drink water and make me feel middle-aged as I pour my third cup. They tell me about some kids they have seen, out at the playground early.

"We stopped at the schoolyard to do our stretching, and there were these two little girls," says Jam, swinging his arms around the kitchen as if he doesn't know what to do with all his animal strength. Jam is taller than Hector, with a wavy mop of fair hair that should be ridiculous, but somehow manages to be attractive. He laughs, and can't stop laughing. Bending over, snorting, he starts Hector off. They've been giggling about this all the way home along the river path. "Well, they weren't that little," says Jam, regaining his breath. "About eight and ten. And Hector and I were just stretching. I swear I never even looked at them. And then all of a sudden the older girl goes all rigid and points at us – at me, really – and shouts, 'Look out! A stranger!' And they hightail it off to their house, I guess, which is the one right beside the schoolyard. 'Look out! A stranger!' What could have brought it on?"

Hector is wiping the sweat off his face with a tea towel, but I don't say anything. I know he is not uncouth enough to put it back into kitchen use, but will hurl it down the basement steps towards the laundry room. His grin is huge, and I find it infectious. I don't quite see why this episode is so hilarious, but I am smiling nevertheless. Little Max dances around between the three of us, weaving in and out happily. He likes having everyone around, talking, doing nothing in particular.

"It's because I took my shirt off, and they were overcome, even they in their very youthful youthfulness," says Hector.

"Oh, you did not," I say, and take in his entire body

with my still tired eyes. He makes my headache disappear. Hector and I have always noted that hangovers, if they are not too debilitating, are arousing. We have various theories about this. He says that it is because you think you are dying, and you feel the need to populate the world quickly before you shuffle off. I say that orgasms contain tiny elements that I have called *fine-golds,* for no particular reason, which are analgesics and also rehydrate key areas of the brain. I smile at him and try to send my thoughts to him, telepathically. "You never take your shirt off."

"True." Hector heads towards the coffee maker to put on another pot, and I am strangely relieved. All this healthy behaviour this morning, getting up early, running, drinking water, has been unnerving. But the Hector who needs a whole bunch of coffee is the one I recognize. I am getting him back. There is no doubt that this visit of Jam's has been far better than past ones, but still there is a constant pulling, this way and that, between us. We vie for Hector. I don't know if Jam is aware of this, but I am keenly so.

I remember the lighter. Years ago, when Jam was visiting us after a long trip to Europe, he brought out with a great flourish the gift he had brought for me. Hector was happily sifting through his pile of gifts: ties, posters, a tiny bust of Buxtehude. Jam presented me with a small lighter. I have never smoked. I didn't understand the gift then. I don't understand it now. It shouldn't bother me. Such a small thing, but the lighter memory still sets my teeth on edge.

The phone rings. The men ignore it, as they always do, so I pick it up. It is, strangely, Beatrice Haight, at just after nine in the morning, on a July Saturday. Her voice is as imperious as usual, but her request, if it came from anyone else, would be rather plaintive. The other difficult older woman in our Department, Jean Smothers, like Beatrice also single, has been staying with Beatrice while her house is being completely painted, inside and out. But now Beatrice has a burst pipe in her house, and an entire floor is flooded, including the guest bedroom. Would I, could I, possibly take on Jean? I find the idea dismaying but have no real reason to say no. True, we only have the second Hide-A-Bed in the second-floor office, but we are going away on Monday and Jean could have the whole place to herself. It would be the decent thing to do.

"Janet." Beatrice's voice is grey. I can picture her on the other end of the line. Grey blouse, grey shoes, grey skirt. No, it's only nine. Grey housecoat. Grey wrapper? What is a wrapper? I try to imagine Beatrice in a negligee, not grey, and wearing those fancy little slippers with heels and bits of feathery pompom on them. Mules? Are those mules? I throw in a boa. Or what about sweatpants? Definitely not. She is speaking. I transfer my attention to her voice.

"Janet. I am appreciative. You will..." She hesitates. "You will enjoy Jean's company, I am assured." Why does she talk like this? I make the appropriate positive noises and the conversation is over. She was doing her damnedest to be a human being, I could tell, but the voice was so papery. Despite the personal nature of the call, I feel as if Beatrice were about to staple my head. I always see her like that: with a big grey stapler at the ready.

I come back to tell Hector about all this, and find

Jam deep into a complicated anecdote about a progressive rock band he did some sound engineering for. "These guys," Jam says and starts to laugh so much that he begins to cough, "these guys were incredible. The hair! It was like the nineties had never happened. Hell, it was like the eighties had never happened. You wanted to ask them if they'd heard that new far-out Pink Floyd record, *Dark Side of the Moon*. But I never needled them. I was broke at the time and these guys had a real following, and they had money. I never lived so well as for those few weeks, until I couldn't stand their noise any more. Man, they paid well, and I had all the freebie beer and steak I could handle – and silk shirts. Those guys had some pet menswear company that kept sending them those really shiny shirts in bright colours, and they'd give heaps of them to me."

Hector and I have never heard about this gig, which is amazing, since we have heard so many of Jam's stories. I wonder if they are always true, but Hector believes them absolutely. I am beginning to feel self-conscious standing there in my nightgown. Jam never looks twice at me, but I am afraid that Little Max will flip the skirt up on one of his happy, careening zooms around the kitchen. But I don't want to leave yet, to shower. I want to hear Jam's story. He tells all his stories with great expressiveness, his arms thrown wide at key moments, doing uncanny imitations of all sorts of voices.

"The lead singer had a throaty, woofing kind of voice that was impossible to deal with in the mixing room. Some people liked it, but I couldn't stand it. These guys had only one album before I tried to mix this second one, and I guess that second album eventually came out, but I could never bear to listen to it. And then they sort of faded from view. Not surprising to me. His voice! I once muttered behind his back that in the liner notes he should be listed as 'Lead Catarrh,' and I think he heard me, but as he didn't know what it meant, he couldn't say anything."

I smile and head off to the shower, nodding at Hector and pointing at Little Max, who has taken off his pants and is rolling on the kitchen floor, visibly inviting everyone to look at his little penis with delight. The cats dodge his kicking legs, but lurk, hoping to pick up the bits of stray toast with Cheez Whiz that fly around Jam's vicinity while he is eating and telling his stories. What am I going to do with Jean Smothers, even for a short while? I know how to behave around Beatrice, who is very orderly; you merely need to fall into line with her plan for the moment. But Jean is the oldest faculty member in our Department, and rather strange in her crotchets. I have never known how to handle her. She once tried to make me part of a team-teaching experiment for a course in Changing Definitions of Realism, and I declined. I couldn't see how we would get past the first half-hour. "Hi, kids. Realism. Yeah. Hmmm. Well, impossible to define. Let's break for coffee." Jean was disappointed in what she seemed to consider my defection, and although no one else stepped up and the course was never taught, she has been reserved in her dealings with me ever since.

I get dressed and come back downstairs to find that Jam is reading *A Fish Out of Water* to Little Max. This is one of their favourites, for different reasons. Little

Max likes the danger of the story. You feed a fish too much, and it grows impossibly big, too big for every pot in the house, too big for the bathtub, too big for the town's swimming pool. It shows no signs of stopping. Possibly this fish is the end of the known world; perhaps this fish will swell to occupy the entire universe. This delights my child, with his apocalyptic streak. He also loves the joyously hopeful/hopeless repetition of it, with the boy certain each time he puts the fish in a new receptacle that this time the tumult is over. Even the youngest reader knows, somehow, that of course the new pots do not mean that the problem is solved, and that with each repetition the problem becomes both more grave and more delightful. For Jam, the book is much simpler. He is certain that it is about masturbation, and as he reads he widens his eyes at me over the top of the book, letting his mouth drop open occasionally in mock horror and dismay.

"Janey, listen to this. Can you believe this? And what happens when Mr. Carp is in that pool with the giant fish, Janey? What is going on?"

"Max," I say. "Remember not to pay any attention to your Uncle Jam." Max does not look at me for the moment, and they go on reading.

I realize that it felt odd just now to speak to them, as if I had not yet spoken today. But that cannot be true. I review the morning. I spoke on the phone; I asked Max not to push me over; I spoke to Hector earlier. I have not said much, but I have spoken. Why do I feel like there is something strange about my voice?

I find Hector shaving, and tell him about Beatrice's broken pipes and the onset of Jean Smothers. He listens, sighing a little, but doesn't say much. He agrees with me that our cottaging makes it impossible not to loan out our house, even to the eccentric Jean, who has been known to smoke a pipe. As he shaves, with a straight razor and much splashing, his eyes look darker than usual. I sit on a stool in the bathroom, watching him, something I like to do. Even as he clears away some of his holiday growth of beard, he still looks swarthy and masculine and rugged, larger than usual, bursting with vital strength. I feel small beside him, a dun-coloured sparrow.

"I haven't had much of a chance to talk with you since Jam came," I say suddenly. I had no intention of saying this, and indeed I had not realized that there was an issue to talk about until a moment ago. I clear my throat and look at him in the mirror. "I feel like I don't talk at all any more, now that I think about it. Like if I did say something, no one would want to listen to me anyway."

Hector has an inscrutable look on his face. He listens patiently but not very sympathetically, or so it seems to me.

"Jam looms so large. He talks all the time. I feel like my role – even your role – is just to listen." I try to make my voice calm and mature, but it is beginning to sound whining. I stop and look again for some sort of response that would comfort me. Hector is quiet, and then there is a crash downstairs, and we are both hurtling through the house to see what it is.

Jam and Little Max have been playing a combination of volleyball and soccer in the living room, with cushions, and a shot has rebounded off the sideboard, knocking over a nearly empty bottle of Silent Sam vodka, which has broken, and a nearly full bottle of red wine, which has not. I look at the situation from a doorway for a bit, but the other three are in a state of not very repentant hilarity that I can't share, and Hector has the cleanup in hand, so I wander off.

I head into the upstairs office and close the door and answer some emails from colleagues I have asked to work with me on starting an online journal. Some people are on holidays, but surprisingly many of them respond to my queries anyway. They must be like me, I think, finding it less stressful to keep working than to figure out how to live at peace with vacationing families. Also surprisingly, many of them are willing to be involved, although nearly all of them try to talk me out of my organizational framework. I had decided that I would like to try for a joint Canadian-British contemporary literature journal, with Canadians writing about Brits and vice versa. I have found it hard to articulate why I have started off this way, and other academics aren't thrilled with my rubric. But if we open it up to contemporary stuff that is Canadian and British, or even European, more generally, without nailing down who is allowed to write about whom, I can get some of them on board. They agree with me that there aren't enough publishing venues for a particular kind of academic work these days. Some of the general journals have shut down. Regular publishing is too expensive. Hector opens the office door, and I look up guiltily. I have been writing emails for over an hour, and it is Saturday morning in summer holidays.

"Come on," he says. "Let's make hot dogs and then go to the beach."

"I thought you couldn't leave town yet. I thought you were waiting for the last draft of your Departmental review thing to be done, and then you were going over it again with the other faculty."

"Nope," he says. "Didn't I tell you? We had Chantal finesse the document last week, and she is such a great little editor that we actually finished the thing early and sent it away to the externals. We're done. It was amazing really."

"No," I say. "You didn't tell me." And he is gone, searching for bathing suits. I can hear Jam downstairs, yelling about where his flask has gone. He wants to fill it up for the beach trip.

I meet Hector again a few moments later in the kitchen. He is dumping wieners in boiling water, and Jam is slicing cheese. I would rather not talk in front of Jam just now, but I do anyway. "I don't think I'm going to go to the beach, if that's okay with you," I say, and look at Hector's face intently. Again, I cannot read it. "I'm going to get things ready for Jean Smothers. And do laundry before we go to the cottage. Can you manage without me, with Little Max, I mean? You remember that time he chased that seagull nearly off the pier, trying to get back a french fry?"

"Oh, Janey. You should come." Hector says it first, but then Jam picks up Hector's line and repeats it, and then sings it. He sings it like Bette Midler, like Caruso, like Tiny Tim, like Anne Murray, like Hank Williams. It is one of his many party tricks. He does it well.

"Oh, Janey. You should come." Little Max appears in the kitchen doorway, and I see that he is still not completely dressed. He has on underpants and a pyjama top. His eyes follow Jam, cavorting around the kitchen with a paring knife, memorizing his every move. "Oh, Janey. You should come." Now Jam is doing a full Freddie Mercury impression, and Little Max is picking up on the stunt, copying him. He begins to sing. I look over at Hector, trying to send him a message with my eyes. But I'm not even sure myself what the message is, and if it arrives it is surely scrambled. Hector laughs at the others, gives me a lopsided smirk and opens the fridge to look for relish.

I HAVE TO EXPLAIN MYSELF TO HECTOR. I wake and it is dark, and he is not in bed. I know it. I lie there, shaking from my dream. I have to explain to Hector. I have to – what? – apologize, I think. In my dream I have been giving an interview to *The New Yorker* and apparently I am so famous that everyone is interested in my private life. "What about family life, Janet Erlicksen? Is it difficult, given your status? What does family mean to you?" And I launch into a highly intimate and detailed examination, for all the world to read, of my qualms about motherhood and marriage. About the lack of privacy. About the impossibility of finding the right number of times a week to have sex with one's spouse. The lack of gratitude from children. About the impossibility of ever understanding, totally, another human being. About my regret that my affair with Nicole Kidman ever became public knowledge. Here my dream becomes less meaningful for a while. There is an interlude where I am wearing nothing but the bottom half of my sister Kyla's figure-skating outfit from a winter carnival in 1972 and I am lost in a maze in a Starbucks, coming back to the counter over and over to try to place the same order for a tall non-fat latté. Over and over. Or is it the same counter? Sometimes it is closed, and sometimes it is staffed but they ignore me or seem unable to see me somehow. The baristas keep changing. They are all unfriendly. I cannot figure out how to leave this Starbucks.

Then I am back doing the interview, and as I wake up I can clearly hear myself saying, "Life with a family and life without a family are both untenable."

Both this final remark and the Starbucks maze are terribly frightening, and I turn to get comfort from Hector, even if he is in one of his deep, deep sleeps. But he is not there. I look at the clock; it is three thirty. The house is silent.

He and Jam went for a martini to Rae and Jerry's about eleven, and I went to bed. They dressed up like Rat Pack members, with skinny ties and conservative suit jackets. They love the lounge at Rae and Jerry's; they like to vie over who is Frank and who is Sammy. Neither likes to be Dean, although occasionally they assign the role to me (my function is to be as loutish as possible), and no one is ever Peter Lawford. "Peter Lawford!" Jam will yell. "Did you see him try to sing in *Easter Parade?* With that angel Judy Garland on his arm, pretending she wasn't dying of embarrassment?"

I lie there for a while and think about my dream, and then, at four fifteen, I hear them enter the house. I expect boisterousness but they are fairly quiet. Hector comes to bed soon and I ask if everything is all right.

Hector laughs, a small laugh through his nose that

is reserved for a particular kind of amusement origi-
nating in Jam's escapades. "Jam," Hector begins
dramatically but sleepily, "has done something to his
collarbone. Probably broken it. We've been in the
emergency for a couple of hours. They couldn't do
much really, so they sort of immobilized the area as
best they could, and he's supposed to go back in
tomorrow."

Below us, in the office, I hear Jean Smothers rise
from the Hide-A-Bed, open the door noisily and scam-
per with an amazing childlike quality to the toilet. I
wonder why. Is it that – and here I wonder why my
imagination works in this manner – she is naked, and
she is moving fast to avoid detection? She arrived this
evening as I was putting Little Max to bed at eight, the
child wild· with exhaustion after a day in the sun and
far too much sugar. I showed her where she could sleep,
and then she trundled up and down the stairs for what
seemed like hours, bringing in truckloads of books
apparently essential to her existence at all times. I saw
the complete works of Galsworthy come up, and I
would not think they were essential to anyone's existence. I had difficulty getting Little Max to stay down,
and didn't emerge from his room for the final time until
nine forty-five. Her stair-climbing, which had not
helped in getting Max settled, had just ended.

Jean Smothers is a tiny and strangely attractive
woman, with wiry grey hair that she keeps short and
tied up with gorgeously tinted long scarves. I have no
idea how old she is, although she cannot be more that
sixty-five or the university would be starting to scoop
her towards the door. She loves teaching, and her energy

shows no signs of flagging. She is infamous for once having been, apparently, the lover of Stephen Sondheim. And Leonard Cohen. Perhaps even Sting, when his name was just Gordon, although I have only heard that at third hand. The Sondheim liaison would seem to be impossible, but she is adamant. About Cohen she will say nothing, but her smiles are positively sphinx-like. Strangely enough, Sting is the easiest to believe. While Hector and Jam puttered about in the basement music studio, drunkenly working out a Beach Boys tune in the style of Arvo Pärt, I half-heartedly offered Jean some tea or wine, at the same time moving sideways towards the stairs to the third floor. My sanctuary. Where I could think about what had happened today. What *had* happened today? Something had, but I could not put my finger on it. She declined, but pressed a book on me. A novel by Ford Madox Ford. I could not imagine anything less comforting to me now, but smiled and nodded and made my escape. Instead I read *Villette* until I fell asleep, waiting for Hector and Jam's return.

"He broke his collarbone? How?"

"We don't know it's broken. We...uh, we were at the Burton Cummings Community Centre, trying to steal an E."

"What?"

"At midnight, Jam thought it would be a useful task to take an E from the sign at the Burton Cummings Community Centre. He stood on the roof of the car and was pulling the letter off the sign when he slipped and fell. He got the letter."

"And then you took him to emerg."

"Yeah."

"Is he okay?"

"Oh, sure. Jam feels no pain. Even when he's sober, which he's not, he feels no pain. I think the guy has no nerves."

I feel like there is an obstacle of some sort between Hector and me, and I should quit talking to him to teach him a lesson, but I need to know. "Why the E?"

Hector does his nose laugh again. "I really don't know. I think he wanted it to be a subtle crime that might not be noticed for a while. If he had turned the sign into the Burto Ummings Community Centre, it would have been too flashy."

"Where is it?"

"He's got it in bed with him. It's really quite big, you know. He's getting very fond of it."

The first thing that enters my mind at this point is that this escapade makes Jam useless as a helper with Little Max at the cottage. He has been wonderful with him so far and gives Hector and me breathing room to read and write and think and do music a bit. So I have told René that we don't need him while we go to the cottage. This was good, because he had signed up for an animation workshop at the art gallery anyway. But I know that caring for Little Max takes all the limbs and stamina an adult can assemble, and now Jam is short an arm.

I think of saying something about this to Hector, but don't. He is quiet, and his breath is becoming regular. Then, before he falls asleep, he chuckles again and mutters, "Jam met a beautiful woman at the bar. Quite taken with her. Blanche Grimm. The least grim woman ever. Fabulous black hair. Very smart. You'd like her."

I do like her, I think of saying. I realize I am holding

conversations with Hector in my head for the first time in all our years together, and not actually voicing them. I told Hector about Blanche, I'm sure. Surely he knows she is in my Department, and it was my idea to get her together with Jam anyway. Does no one listen to me? Do I not exist?

Hector is asleep, and I am wide awake. I am afraid to enter the possibility of the frightening Starbucks dream again. Both cats, who defected two weeks ago to Jam's bed when he arrived, suddenly arrive and climb up beside me. Adele curls in around my knees, and Helen heads for my pillow. I push her down between Hector and me, and they go to sleep. Jam's large metal E must have put them off.

Or they know there is something wrong with me. The cats always know when I am sick. If anyone is sick. They arrive and lie uncharacteristically still beside anyone in distress. I was not aware that I was really in that much distress, but now I am spooked, and review all the unpleasant aspects of the day in my mind again. At six I finally go to sleep, after hearing the Beach Boys sing "Wouldn't it Be Nice" over and over in my memory because the guys were fooling around with it in the basement studio. I wake again at nine thirty, when Little Max comes in, blissfully latish, rested and cheerful from sleeping in.

I resolve to be more amiable today, and this lasts until ten thirty, when I hear from Jam that they met not only the beautiful Blanche at the lounge at Rae and Jerry's, but also the lovely Chantal. Apparently Chantal and Blanche have met at the university and hit it off. Unusually, the two raven-haired beauties don't mind being seen in each other's company, not requiring the usual ordinary woman as dramatic contrast. They had a drink together with Jam and Hector, although the young women declined to be part of the E episode.

I feel a tightness in my chest that I can tell no one about. Because its source is both real and not real. Part of me knows there is no danger, but another part of me is adamant that there is.

The guys are settling into the kitchen, making a complicated brunch dish they have read about in *GQ*, and ogling the photos of semiclad starlets while pretending to consult the recipe. Little Max is helping them crack eggs, which he will never do for me. Jean is smoking her pipe and drinking coffee in the backyard. Mosquitoes do not bite her. I look at the clock. It is ten forty-five and I feel like I am having an asthma attack, except I don't have asthma and don't know what an asthma attack would feel like if I did have one.

"I'm going to church. Okay? Okay, guys? I'll be back at noon." Hector kisses me and nods, smiling. He rubs his nose in my hair, and then pulls me to him, hard, and pushes his nose around towards the back of my head. He likes the scent of me there, he always says. He holds me, and breathes in and out.

"Okay," he says. He smiles again. "Give Laurel a kiss for me." Laurel is the summer minister, a young seminarian who is probably a lesbian, although she doesn't appear to know it. Little Max pulls at my sundress for a moment, but then goes off to watch Jam wind his tensor bandage around his upper body. I am released. I speed past Jean, towards the car, waving at her, saying I'll be back soon. I never invite friends to church. I know you're supposed to, but I can't.

I GET TO CHURCH AND PULL INTO the sparsely populated parking lot. July. No one in Winnipeg goes to church in July. Except losers. It is not Laurel, but our regular minister, Jake, who has come back from one half of his holidays. I am glad to see him, to soak in his warm and forgiving nature. I sit through the service, paying only half a mind to the scriptures, singing with reserve. And then I hear a line, in Psalm Eighty-four, that cracks something open in me, and I'm glad I'm sitting near the back, because I am quietly and discreetly (I hope) crying. I don't know why.

For a day in your courts is better than a thousand elsewhere.

Jake can see that I'm crying, and I don't mind. He looks my way and nods imperceptibly. I don't know why I am crying.

GIRLS AGAINST THE BOYS

I AM READING MY WAY THROUGH THE NOVELS OF Charlotte Brontë, mostly, I think, so I can feel superior to her. I wonder how many academics do this, choose projects that make them feel smarter through some process of comparison. Not that Brontë wasn't smart. But the chaos of a novel like *Villette*. Come on. Get it together, woman. How many scenes of delirium, how many doubled and halved identities can there be in one novel? Intriguing as a psychoanalytic case study; a mess as a novel.

Jam is gone. Jean is gone. We are done our holidays. I feel great relief, although I must say my tan this year is the best I've ever had. The weather at the cottage was great, and Jam, it turned out, was as capable of playing with Little Max as before. He did more things with his feet; there was constant soccer, constant foot drumming. He and Little Max and Hector worked on a foot-drumming ensemble everyday, using whatever came to hand (to foot, I mean): plastic beach buckets, Frisbees, beer boxes. They got to be pretty good. Little Max can be extraordinarily disciplined for a three-year-old, when he wants to be. The cottage was small, so I felt exposed a lot, and Jam's huge personality took up most of the space. I was anxious about making love with Hector there, although he didn't seem to notice that the other two were on the other side of a wall as substantial as a lasagna noodle.

Little Max is back at daycare. I am preparing my fall syllabi. Hector is finishing a manuscript about Buxtehude. He gets caught up in these projects and listens to the music of the period obsessively. He wants to rename our cats, give them more Baroque names. Wilhelmina and Frederica. Or maybe Ludmilla.

Before Jam left, we had Blanche over for a barbeque. She was a charming but quiet guest, although Jam eventually got her laughing quite a bit. It turns out she wants to help me with the campus peace movement stuff in the fall. She was wearing a white cotton peasant blouse, the kind I never wear because without being ironed it makes me look like a crumpled Kleenex. Hers was crisp and lovely, and she had a long skirt in variegated shades of blue, and enigmatic little sandals, probably Italian. Simple. Gorgeous. Infuriating. I sought in her face traces of makeup and could find none this time. This makes no sense. No one could look that beautiful without makeup. I know this. I am not a fool. But if she uses makeup, I cannot see how.

I have coffee with Tom, who has returned from a canoeing trip up north. The top of his bald head is bright red and his nose is peeling. He stretches out his long legs and shows me developments in his calf muscles that make him extremely proud. He tells stories of bears that climb trees to get at his stash of beer and cookies, tells of a couple he met who were desperately waiting for a plane to take them back south. They cut their trip radically short when they realized that the bags of supplies they thought would be their lifeline for a rugged two weeks in the isolated north turned out to be their recycling, and most of their clothes and food and insect repellent were in similar bags in their back lane. They had radioed to be picked up, and had only spent thirty-six hours in the north, and were a little chagrined by their inability to make a go of it. They were long-legged, hiking-boot-wearing Scandinavian types. Tom describes them with his usual relish, giving them the appellations Odin and Freya. He loves it when gods come tumbling to earth.

Tom wants to talk about two things, as we settle into our second cappuccino of the morning at the Neighbourhood Café. I try not to think about Max at daycare, try to think of this meeting with Tom as work. Which it is, in a way. One of the things he wants to discuss is Beatrice's decadence conference, coming up in September, and any intervention we may want to plan. None of us is presenting papers, although Hector is slated to be part of a group playing John Adams and Steve Reich pieces, and I am to chair a session. But Tom desperately wants to hijack the conference in some fun way, although I find mostly that I want to listen to his plans and not think about this too much. I have known Tom since we were undergrads together in the eighties and he signed up for the same aerobics class as I did in the university athletic centre. He was the only man in a room full of young women, but he studiously ignored all of us. He threw himself into aerobics with a crazed and clumsy delight. I have never seen anything like it before or since. He was so awful that it was distracting for me and I dropped the class. But we picked up a friendship that has never lapsed. And never will, unless I press him too closely on his private life or flash him too much of mine.

Tom also wants to know about Jam and Blanche. He knows them both, although not well, and finds them both fascinating. He wants to know what they got up to. Jam is programmed to tumble into bed with almost all the attractive women he meets, and Blanche is the most attractive woman whom any of us have met in a long time. But she seems so inviolable and distinctly independent somehow, like a goddess not in need of human companionship.

"But they did disappear after supper. Did I tell you that?" I take a bite out of a biscotti, a snack I do not even like much, but I have to have something to chew on. "Hector and I were mixing drinks and putting food away, and we came out on the porch, and they had gone. On a walk, apparently. But they were gone for nearly an hour, and when they came back they were...well, weird. Jam was terribly subdued, for him, I mean. He told off-colour stories about Ray Charles and all that, but I'd heard them before, and his heart wasn't in it. She seemed remote and pure and beautiful. And then she went home about eleven. And Jam went for another walk until the wee hours."

Tom drums his fingers on the table. He lives vicariously through other people's romances and scrapes, having no interest in getting his hands dirty with affairs of his own. He was married as a very young man, before I met him, and it lasted only six months. He has only spoken of it once or twice. Whatever happened, it was enough. "Was she at all mussed up when she came back from the walk?"

"Nope. She still looked perfect. I really don't think anything happened, Tom. Mighty Jam has struck out." Tom and I smirk at each other. We like Jam well enough, most of the time, but we tire of Hector's loving loyalty to the guy. At least I think that's what is going on. We don't articulate things like that, Tom and I. I speculate that we are both in love with Hector and equally resent sharing him with Jam. My theory is that Tom is not jealous of me because he sees me not as Hector's wife but as his sister somehow. I don't know. "And then later that week Jam went back to Ottawa. I guess that's that."

Tom wants to talk more about the harmonium scheme, but I refer him to Hector, since I really know nothing about harmoniums. Harmonia? Tom needs to know how heavy they are. How hard to fit through doors. What Scriabin would sound like played on a harmonium. Or Scott Joplin. But I am unable to answer any of these questions. I like the sound of the word harmonium, but that's as far as I've got. I get up and hug Tom. I realize I hardly ever hug anyone. I have an appointment at eleven.

I am going to see Jake, our minister. This is our second meeting. After I spent that Sunday morning last month crying, Jake offered to meet with me once a week, on Mondays. I haven't mentioned this to Hector yet, which feels very strange indeed. I tell Hector everything, but I don't really know why I am meeting Jake. I have a feeling it might have something to do with our marriage, and I want to get a handle on it first. But maybe it doesn't. I'm not sure. I just feel grief. Of some sort. I try out the different words to myself when I am alone. Grief. Suffering. Despair. Anguish. They are all too much. I have no reason to be grieving. None. This is a good life. There is no suffering involved. But then I hit on the word *mourning*, and I feel something. That is the discovery I am taking to Jake today.

NEXT WEEK IS OUR ANNUAL Department retreat, to a local Bible camp for a day. We do this every year in late August, ostensibly to get energized for the year, to orient new faculty and staff, to be together in relaxing circumstances. But these things never seem to work out, for me anyway. Some people seem to have a great time, playing Frisbee golf and croquet and doing archery. I want to crawl off into a corner with a book, but this appears to be the opposite of what I am supposed to do. The women go for walks together, earnestly discussing things I don't get, taking long strides, nodding at each other. I often end up on the fringes of the little duos and trios of introverts working on five-hundred-piece jigsaw puzzles with lots of sky. I don't do the puzzles – I'm not that introverted – but I watch for a while and experience more fellow feeling than I do with the archery people and the walkers.

But it turns out that more people than me are a little dissatisfied with these retreats, and so I have been put on the planning committee for this latest venture. Our intention is, supposedly, to reshape the retreat experience. I am enough of a realist or a pessimist to know that, whatever we do, the retreats will never change much. I suggested early on a change of venue. I find the idea of all these self-important post-structuralists and sceptical narratologists and cranky linguists getting together at Camp Elijah ridiculous. But the camp is cheap and the food edible.

This year, we are going to do more things as a large group. This is not my idea, but I have been overridden by Beatrice, Jean and Ivan, our Department's medievalist. In planning meetings, of which we have had far too many for such a minor event, the three of them have bonded, and I have taken to calling them, in my mind, The Three Horsepersons of the Apocalypse. For no particular reason.

It is afternoon and I arrive late at the planning meeting. I have been at The Bay, looking at slips that Hector would like to see me in, and I lost track of time. This is supposed to be the last meeting, and they are already deep into a discussion of mixers. The kind of get-to-know-you game that I find excruciating. I realize I was supposed to research these but have repressed the memory of this. So, in the absence of what might have been my more sensible suggestions, the other three have already fastened on a find of Ivan's. It is a kind of intellectual Twister that he has dug up somewhere. I can barely follow the instructions, but I am no good at games. It involves answering literary trivia questions, one by one, and then, depending on one's success, one moves one's seat, which will be colour-coded, so that we all eventually sit beside people we don't normally sit with. Whenever a seat is changed, the action stops and the person we have moved to sit beside gets to ask us a question about some matter in our lives that probably has been hitherto completely unknown. This question and answer period is public and unpredictable, and I find the whole thing appalling. The prospect of both professional and personal humiliation lurks here in the two aspects of this awful game. But the others are eager to do it, and I open and close my mouth uncertainly on my protest. What is it that I am protesting? It always takes me awhile to sort out my feelings about such things, and by then I have been flattened by someone's juggernaut.

Then they're on to group games that don't allow the

guys to wander off in one direction and the girls in another. This is Jean's description. In my imagination, the Department's women parade past. I cannot think of any of them as girls. Luckily, those kids' cooperative parachute games have already been considered and rejected – the kind where a huge, colourful circle of parachute cloth is placed on the ground, and everyone scuttles under it and does something. I've never been sure what. But The Three have fastened on beach volleyball as a good possibility. There are equal numbers of men and women in the Department, and so "girls against the boys" is in order. Volleyball is declared to be accessible to everyone, even the somewhat overweight Ivan, and not too demanding in the skill department. "And we will be together, which is our goal," says Beatrice, and checks something off on the list in front of her.

Beatrice has also decided that we will decorate cookies together, and that there will be a prize for the cookie that best exemplifies the spirit of the Department. I cannot think there is a spirit in the Department, unless it is thinly disguised enmity or alienation. Nausea? When I arrived, the Department was divided into cultural studies people plus feminists against everyone else, and I never could understand the divide or sort out which side I was supposed to be on. Soon it became clear that the reasons for the divide were unimportant. There had to be a divide, a constant threat of skirmish, to please the battlers in the Department, who were in the minority but were nevertheless a powerful minority. Beatrice is one of them. She doesn't feel alive, I reckon, unless she has a couple of scholarly feuds on the boil.

Jean is not really one of them, so I wonder at the way she is going along with Beatrice lately. Jean is usually an individual, unpredictable. Ivan I cannot get a bead on. He is new enough that he is a puzzle to me still, but I find his behaviour so far rather unprofessional. At one point he suggests a bathing beauty contest, and he doesn't seem entirely facetious. I decide, silently, that I would like black icing for my cookie, and wonder if there will be some provided.

I note with some relief that Jean is not as unlike herself today as I had thought. Absent-mindedly she is fishing in her jacket pocket and brings out her pipe. She sticks it between her teeth. I don't think she even realizes she is doing this. Beatrice does. The pipe is not lit, of course, but Beatrice's jaw stiffens, her eyes narrow.

A picture in my mind's eye of Beatrice Haight in an orange bikini and a little thong swims into view, and I have to stare at my coffee cup for a long time to get myself under control. "Janet, dear, what do you think of the community crossword idea?" Beatrice's lips are pursed. It is August. It is hot, but Beatrice does not have a hair out of place. There is no perspiration anywhere on her body, and she is wearing a navy blue suit that looks suitable for a meet-and-greet with the Queen Mother.

I have not heard the community crossword idea. Jean looks across the table at me, speculatively and rather kindly, and explains. She puts her pipe away. There will be a huge crossword puzzle projected on the wall of the dining hall and we will work on it together, in a kind of delightful verbal scrimmage. I nod. Sure, whatever. Jean was nice to us about the use of our house last month. She said nothing about the state of our towels, the ones we've had since before we were married, and left one of those enormous cookie bouquets on the dining-room table. The ideal present. I ate most of the cookies.

I escape from the meeting, having agreed to everything they wanted and having put forward no ideas of my own. I think the retreat will be revolting and briefly consider feigning illness on the day. But I cannot. I am on the planning committee. I am responsible. I remind myself that I like being responsible.

I head past the bucket outside Biology. The leaking ceiling has not been fixed. I duck into my office and shut the door. It is dark in there, the blinds pulled against the late-summer sun. I feel comfortable in my office, even though it is filled with reminders of things I do not have ready for the start of classes in ten days. I sit at my desk and pull out the journal I have started to keep so that I can track things I am discussing with Jake.

Jake has said remarkably little about my weeping, or about anything. He asked a few general questions about family and work and health, and then laid out a little plan of conversation, meditation, reflective reading and writing. He does not, I am relieved to find out, use the word "journaling." This is not a word. He treats me cautiously, but affably, with respect. He seems to find me more interesting than I do myself. I want to talk about Hector and the baby, but Jake steers away from them for now. They seem not to interest him. They interest me. Jake wants to find out what's bothering me, and he doesn't seem to think it's either of them. I say "seem" because Jake, like all good ministers and counsellors, doesn't say too much. He doesn't commit. He's a listener; he's there. He prompts me a little, but very little.

I open my journal and read over the first few pages. I start off rather self-consciously with a line of questioning. Am I afraid of aging? Why do I have so few female friends? Do I feel inadequate among my colleagues and if so, why? Am I afraid that Hector will have an affair with someone? With Chantal, for in-stance? Then there's a bit about my father and the way he ignored my mother. But this doesn't bother me any more. I have scribbled a bunch of stuff like this for a while, and then over the page I have jotted phrases, randomly.

Crystal Palace
Hubris
Sinners
The way my first Bible smelled
Wool pants paralysis

These are either story titles I have played with over the years and never written, or sense memories I intend to work into something. The wool pants paralysis is the most vivid. I was about ten, maybe, and my mother had sewn me some wool pants, and they bothered me so much that I ended up lying down on the nurse's cot at school, unable (or unwilling) to move my legs. I was very tall for my age, and the nurse talked about growing pains, yet I knew that was not it. But I didn't correct her. I felt secure lying there, waiting for the end of the school day, when I would move slowly to the school bus and move as little as possible all the way home, and never wear those pants again. My mother did not know that I was sensitive to wool. How could she?

But what am I supposed to do with this memory?

IT IS MONDAY MORNING AGAIN, the last week of

August, and I settle onto Jake's worn couch and stare at his Celtic cross, his Chagall prints. And then I say something I have not prepared in the least. "I cannot – cannot – stop thinking about..." I say the name. It is the name of a well-known rapist and murderer from at least fifteen years ago. It is a name I have avoided saying or reading or hearing, as if the letters of his name would cut me, contaminate my being. But they have anyway. I have turned aside from this monster for all these years, but the wickedness is as present as it ever was. To me.

Jake looks calmly at me. I realize I am twisting my hands, tearing at little pieces of skin near my fingernails. I really did not know I was going to say this. I try to stop, but can't. "Even before I got pregnant with Max, I had more or less stopped reading newspapers and newsmagazines. We stopped TV reception a long time ago, to save money. And then when I was going to have a child, I found that I really couldn't hear about the horrors on the news. At all. Because inside me there was this unbearably vulnerable creature, and outside there were these...these horrors. The radio tricked me one day. I usually found the CBC Radio news bearable, but one day they played a nine-one-one call from a child whose mother had been stabbed by someone. I – I can't remember the details, but I can remember the tone of the child's voice, so bewildered. And I can remember my outrage. Outrage that the CBC had played this thing, had made me listen to it. For what purpose?"

I can see Jake's eyes on my face. I wonder, at the back of my mind, if he is thinking that the good-natured, joking Janet who is on the stewardship and the church education committees is a fraud, and now he has to deal with the true Janet, this phobic idiot who is apparently searching, willy-nilly, for some way to ruin her pretty damned good life. If he is thinking anything of the sort it does not show.

"Anyway." I take a deep breath and name the murderer again. I know my forehead is furrowed. I can feel it, and I try to smooth it out and pull down my shoulders. They have ended up somewhere in line with my ears, from anxiety, and I realign them, move them back and forth. Jake never looks impatient. "It was impossible to avoid the case. You know? I had to be extra vigilant. It's still everywhere. But I can't know about it. I can't know what he did to those girls. Because it...it interferes with me making love with my own husband. Somehow, whatever was sexual in that man's violence towards those poor dead girls has crept into, tainted, poisoned my...my marital bed. I don't know why. But he had sex with them. And I have sex with Hector. And we're...I don't know...we're all connected somehow, and sometimes this leaps into my mind as I'm making love, making love with the nicest man in the world. And it stops everything. Everything. I get panicky sometimes. This has been going on for a long time. The trial is long over. It's all long over."

Jake shakes his head. "You know, Janey, that what someone like that does is not the same as eroticism. It's not really sex. It's power; it's aggression. It's not sexual, not really. Not like the healthy kind of sexuality we're all supposed to have."

I had thought it would be difficult talking about this with Jake, with anyone, but I find it is not. I feel relieved to be dragging this out into the open. "I know.

I keep saying that to myself. But this horror won't go away. And I get so, *so* angry at the media whenever they discuss it, rather proudly. Our own Canadian sex-crime monster. And the fuss about his looks, as if good looks were somehow supposed to be a guarantee of moral value. There I am, in bed with Hector, and swimming in pools of nausea, and..."

I trail off and look at Jake imploringly. I lift my hands, let them drop. I have said all I can say, but I think it is enough for him to understand. He is silent and thoughtful for a long time, looking out his window, nodding, looking at his cross. I look at it too. Jake scratches behind his ear for a while.

Finally he speaks. "What if you wrote about all this? "Wait –" I have started to protest, instantly. "Hear me out, Janey." He used to call me Janet, but I have asked him to call me Janey, as my friends do. It sounds nice, here in this troubled space I have created in his once-comfortable office. "You could write it as a journal, or a poem, or a letter. You don't have to write the details that bother you. But you should write about the feelings, what he has done to you." I look at him. It seems so obvious, all of a sudden. I had thought I was sickened by what the killer had done to children, and I was, as a mother, as a human being, disturbed by that. But now Jake has realized that this particular murderer had done something to me.

"If I did this," I say, slowly, "then what? What do I do with the letter or the poem or whatever? Well. Not a poem. I cannot make art out of this. I refuse to make art out of this. But what do I do with this document? Do I give it to you?"

He considers. This is not a rote response. He is making it up for me, and I appreciate that. This is not in any of his counselling workbooks, his seminary courses. "Do you want to?"

"I don't know. Maybe. Can I think about that? I don't even know if I can write the thing yet. Do you really think it is a good idea?"

Jake smiles, lopsidedly. He is in his late fifties. He has a little grey beard, but his hair is still brown, curling a little on his shirt collar. He is wearing a green shirt today, with brown shorts, and the colours don't quite go together. But Jake somehow always looks right to me. He is perfectly ordinary, and perfectly comfortable to me. I'm sure he is not ordinary, no one is, but it soothes me to believe it just now. "I'm not sure, I'm really not. I'm sorry. This is a big one. You've been carrying this around for years now. You need to do something fairly big to try to counter it."

"A person can't ever really...really get rid of something like this, can she?" I say. "It can't be forgotten. It shouldn't be forgotten. Right? But if you can't get rid of it, if you can't forget it, what do you do with it?" This is the heart of it, for me. The way the memory of this crime will be with me forever, and it's not even my crime, which makes me feel even sicker. What do real victims and survivors feel? How do they cope? How do parents cope? There is a brief flicker, in my inner cinema, of someone scooping up Little Max, bundling him into a van, speeding off... I am too imaginative. It makes me a good professor, but it's a pain to me as a human being.

I know that Jake will probably say something about forgiveness now, and I am ready with my countering arguments. How can I forgive when I'm not even really involved? Anyway, it's God's job. Too big for me. But Jake doesn't mention forgiveness. He says that if I do decide to write this all down, and he thinks I should because the written language is so much a part of who I am, then I should find some way of sending these manuscripts. To God.

I think of the Dickens novel *Bleak House* all of a sudden. All the characters are connected: intimately, elaborately. And contrary to what the naïve might think, this connectivity causes pain. And in *Mrs. Dalloway*, I think. Suffering. The spread of misery, not its alleviation. Connection.

"You are absolutely in the right to be horrified by this," says Jake slowly. "I am appalled, really, that people recover, publicly, privately, from these things as quickly as they sometimes appear to." He rubs a hand over his head and leans forward on his knees, staring down at his Birkenstocks. "You are not recovering, Janey. That says wonderful things about you. And it's awful that this is getting in the way of loving Hector. An awful thing. I wouldn't want to forgive it either. Maybe human beings can never forgive things like this, not really. But we have to think of something, some way to care for you. Because you are precious, Janey. Yeah, yeah, I know. But you are."

I am crying now, and have been for a while. "You don't allow yourself to be precious, do you?" he asks, quietly. "Just with Hector, probably. Sometimes." I shake my head. I blow my nose, smile at him wearily. I could suddenly sleep, all afternoon.

"I'm supposed to be the funny one," I say, and I get up and shake Jake's hand, and as he always does, he grasps my upper arms instead, and pulls me towards him in a bear hug. It feels like a lame thing to say. *I'm supposed to be the funny one.* But I don't have anything else to say.

"You can be funny again later." He takes my coffee cup. "Let yourself be something else for a while."

I HAVE TAKEN THE BUS TO THE CHURCH and I walk home now, taking my time. It is a great day and everyone who isn't at the beach is out gardening, cutting their lawns, throwing balls to dogs who are wearing kerchiefs around their necks. I walk through the West End and several times see ancient couples puttering around their yards together, painting fences, pulling weeds and pointing at tomatoes. An ancient Portuguese or Italian couple comes towards me. He is walking a little ahead of her. She is overweight and cannot keep up. She walks as best she can, carrying a shopping bag, wearing what was once called a housedress. I wonder where anyone gets them now. I am depressed by the sight of this couple, with him ahead of her, and then, as I have this thought, he stops and looks back at her, and waits for her to come up beside him. Then he takes her hand, and they walk on, slowly. He doesn't take her shopping bag, I notice. But maybe she doesn't relinquish it. Maybe that's it.

THE MAKEOVER

HECTOR IS GOING THROUGH THE IKEA CATALOGUE when I come through the door with the groceries. Little Max is destroying the Lego castle that Hector has made for him, and Hector is pretending to take no notice, which theoretically takes the fun out of the demolition for Max. He does finally stop, and climbs up beside Hector, making Hector turn to the pages with kids' furniture. I dump the bags in the kitchen and come and sit on Hector's other side.

"I missed you."

"I missed you too," he says, and puts his hand on a special place on my thigh that only he knows about. "I haven't seen you for seventy-three minutes."

"I know. It was awful."

"What was awful?" asks Little Max.

"Being away from your papa." I ruffle his hair. "And from you, of course." Max offers his face to me for a kiss, in a gesture inherited from his father. I bend to get the kiss, which is sloppy. "What is so interesting in the IKEA catalogue?" I say and place my fingers, deliberately, on Hector's knee.

"Oh, everything and nothing," says Hector. "I was thinking of replacing all of our old IKEA furniture with almost identical new IKEA furniture. No, really I was thinking of a wedding gift for Chantal."

It turns out that the lovely Chantal has for years been having a low-key affair with one of the city's most lauded church musicians, someone twenty years her senior, and he has finally decided to abandon his glorious bachelorhood. I wish I felt a little better about this news. When I heard it, I thought of marriages in nineteenth-century novels where sweet young things marry well-meaning but oblivious, doddering, much older gentlemen, and the disparity of age somehow makes the woman even more of a prey to bounders and fops than if she had been single.

"You're thinking of buying them shelving units?"

"Nah. I've given up on the Chantal thing. You can work your gift card magic, as per usual. A gift card to one of the usual places, my dear, please." Max pulls the catalogue out of Hector's hands, rips out a page of kids' toys. I open my mouth to say something to Max, but he has already skedaddled out of the room.

"Victoria's Secret, you mean?" I tap my fingers on Hector's knee, meaningfully. This time he looks at my hand, and then up at my eyes, and then down at my hand again.

"Janey, whatever has happened to your hands?"

"Manicure."

"Manicure."

"Yup."

"Janey, you never had a manicure in your life. Whatever possessed you? Where is my wife? Who took my wife? Are you a pod person? Are you a Stepford Wife?"

I grin and stare at the fingernails, which do not seem like mine. They are. I have no extensions, but these nails have nevertheless been prodded and polished and painted so that they are decidedly unfamiliar. I hear Little Max in the kitchen, opening and closing the refrigerator door, singing "Sandwiches are beautiful, sandwiches are fine." He says "sand-itches." I would not allow red nail polish, but there is a pale peach colour on them that I decide is worse. I might as well have gone for hellish red.

"It was a gift," I say. "From Blanche and Jean, for my birthday."

"That makes no sense," says Hector, and I nod.

"I know. And apparently I am booked for a make-over and a spa treatment of some sort. You can come and watch if you want."

"I don't want you made over. I like you the way you are. As you know."

I sigh and feign disinterestedness, but I am rather foolishly excited about the makeover. I will make fun of it, but I have never had anything of the sort and want to know just once what I might look like under Hollywood conditions. When I went to have my official graduation photo taken after my PhD I said to the photographer, only half jokingly, that I wanted to look like Greta Garbo. Instead of smiling or humouring me, he looked at me with such disbelief that it stung. Maybe he'd never heard of Greta Garbo and was merely being ignorant; he was sort of young. But at the time I was just hurt. I meant it to be funny, but I also wanted it to be true. The pictures sucked anyway, and I refused to buy any of them. Jerk. Serves him right. Max comes back into the room. "Poop," he says. "Poop poop poop. Bum."

"Jean and Blanche are doing a joint presentation on all this pointless women's stuff," I say to Hector. "At the decadence conference, and they need someone impartial to go in undercover and experience the thing,

and take notes about how often the spa people try to
convince me that I need to conform to certain sexual
or aesthetic types. You know. I don't know how serious
it is. I think, oddly enough, that they are actually plotting a bit of guerrilla theatre of their own, to shake up
Beatrice's conference. Anyway, it is a birthday gift, and
I have to accept it." Hector is still staring at my nails,
and now Max is too. Max reaches out and taps my
thumbnail, apprehensively. "Hey tiger, what is your
favourite kind of pie?"

"I hate pie." Little Max kicks the coffee table.

"That is not true. You love love love cherry pie. You
ate a whole bunch last time."

"I hate cherry pie."

"Well, I got one, so I guess Papa and I will have to
eat it all."

"Sad," says Hector, and pushes up off the couch, dis-
entangling his legs from a skipping rope and brushing
off many toys: bits from a Barrel of Monkeys and a
Mrs. Potato Head, as well as several My Little Ponies.
I can hear him in the kitchen, unpacking the grocery
bags and smacking his lips at the contents. "Colossal
Jumbo Queen Stuffed Olives. Oooh, Janey." I listen to
his rustling as I lie on the couch under the considerable
weight of Little Max, who has pinned me down with
his own prone body. I lie there, stroking his shoulder
blades and watching his back go up and down with his
breathing. Hector comes to the doorway with a can of
coconut milk in his hand, about to say something, but
stops when he sees us, and watches. He smiles. I am
learning to relax under Max's attentions, which can be
startling and rough. But if I relax into them, things
generally go better. Not always. He climbed onto my

lap when I was on the phone a few days ago, and, even as I was kissing the top of his head, he began to pull my ponytail, rhythmically and hard. I couldn't do anything; I was on the phone to the credit union. By the time I was off the phone, our relationship had deteriorated badly. It took a while for me to recover from that one. He seemed to have forgotten it in minutes.

"Do I see cheese fondue and pina coladas in our future? Near future?" Hector does a little dance in the doorway, and I smile and nod. I want to celebrate. Today I took the third and what I hope is the last of my Missives of Anguish to Jake in his office, and we burned it. The first one we tore up and sailed on the Assiniboine. The second we tore up and let fly from the top of Garbage Hill. We had no set plan of how many documents there might be, but today, seeing the paper burn, I felt the pressure lift, at least in part, and I hope this is the end of it. Hector knows that I have been hoping for this to be the last part, of this stage anyway. He is encouraging me to keep on doing something with Jake, a spiritual book study or something. Maybe I will.

Someone comes to the front door and Little Max catapults off my body and hurtles towards the door. It is René, who walks in quietly and calmly, picking up Little Max's bulk with ease and perching him on one arm, somehow. René has grown about two feet, it seems to me, and he was already taller than either Hector or me when we met him in the spring. The kid is going to be a giant. He has come to borrow some music from Hector, and the three of them disappear into the basement to hunt it up.

Jake and I had no plan to be elemental, but as we

embarked on the wind project at Garbage Hill, I could see the progression. So we still have earth in reserve. Water, air, fire, and earth. We can bury a letter of anger and fear if we want. But I want to show myself that I am on top of this, don't need the full course of treatment. I am stronger than anyone realizes.

The phone rings, and suddenly I realize I have a headache. When did it arrive? I debate whether to pick up the phone – officially it is the supper hour, although we are not eating, and rarely eat at this time – but I am sitting right beside the damned thing. I answer.

"Dr. Janet Erlicksen?"

"Yes."

"This is James Micawber, of Heep and Micawber, and we represent the estate of the Nigerian billionaire Enzio Mullambe, and we would like to be enlightened as to why you have not answered our electronic communications as to the acceptance of a fortune of fifty million pounds sterling that is presently awaiting you in a secret account in Zurich."

"Hi, Jam."

"Hi, Janey. Fifty million pounds. That's quite a lot, Janey. You really should respond."

"Ah, well, you can have it, Jam. Where are you? How are you?"

"I'm in Brandon. Didn't Hector tell you? I'm judging a woodwind thing here, and I'll be done tomorrow, and I fly east on Monday, so I'll be arriving soon and I want you to wear that little transparent sarong thing you wore the first time I met you on the beach at Tahiti."

"That wasn't me. That was a lovely unnamed native girl in *Mutiny on the Bounty,* the movie we were watching the first night I met you."

"Oh yeah. Well, you must have something of that sort."

"Baby baby," I say, and find I am smiling in spite of myself. "Do you want to talk to Hector? He's around here somewhere, being a musical genius."

"Nope. I want to be picked up at the bus depot at eleven fifty-five a.m. tomorrow and I want you to do it. I don't trust Hector. He'll forget about me and wander off to the Gentleman's Club and be there for hours, and I'll be abandoned among the addicts and space aliens and pimply heavy metal fans. It is too terrifying for words. I trust you, Janey. Only you. Bring the tiny tyrant. I miss him, and have been wanting to feed him four pounds of Timbits for ages."

"Okay."

"Actually, you can be thinking about something before then. I want to ask you..." Jam uncharacteristically hesitates, searching for what he wants to say. "I wonder if you've seen much of Blanche Grimm lately."

"Sure, some," I answer. "We're back in session, and we're on a couple of committees together. We went for coffee last week. What about her?"

"I wanted to know what you think of – oh, never mind, maybe I can think more about how to put this and I'll tell you tomorrow." He pauses and his usual voice returns. "Oh, Janey, I'll be bringing a French horn as a present for the kid. Don't worry. He'll pick it up right away and the practising won't be hard to listen to at all."

I get off the phone with Jam and go to the kitchen to take the ready-cooked chicken out of its packaging. This is the best thing ever created, the automatic chicken from Safeway. The other best thing ever created is the birth control pill. Oh, yes, and the VCR (and DVD players too, I guess, but we haven't sprung for one yet). These are the three best things ever created. A perfect evening involves all three of these, and maybe that is what this is going to be.

"HECTOR."

"Hmmm-mmm."

"Are you Heathcliff, do you think? Or Rochester?"

"Are those my two choices?" He is balancing a dish of ice cream and a glass of Scotch on a pillow on top of his stomach. We are in bed. It is midnight. We have had fondue and pina coladas. We have watched old SCTV episodes on crappy old videotapes and then half a Fred and Ginger movie. Then we have tried to make love, but I am skittish, and Hector has good-naturedly backed off and tackled some ice cream. But he is not giving up, and is watching me warmly but not possessively, looking for an opening, an opportunity to be helpful. I know him. He would say it is a pleasure to be helpful to me, and would lick his lips. But he does honestly like to be helpful. "Why can't I be Bill Sykes if I want? Sancho Panza? Spartacus?"

"I don't know. I'm reading the Brontës, that's why. Which one are you?"

"What do you think?"

"Well, Rochester, of course."

"Rochester! Why should I be Rochester? He's a bastard. And he has to be blinded and lose an arm or something before he can be tamed. Tamed! Do I need to be tamed? As if. Tamed! And he's tricky. Why does he dress up like a gypsy to test Jane Eyre? Do you think

I would ever do such a thing?"

"Well, you're more Rochester than Heathcliff. And the gypsy thing is sort of funny. Funnier than anything Heathcliff would ever do."

"Why do I have to be either? Granted, Rochester is less of a bastard. Or is he? Anyway, I'm not either." He takes a sip of his Scotch, and puts his empty ice cream dish on the floor. I am sitting, cross-legged, at the end of the bed. "Is it that you think you are Jane Eyre, and not Cathy, and so you have to match me to you?"

I had not really put it to myself like that, but now that Hector says it, I know it is true. I am matching us in Brontë terms, and I know this is a dangerous game to play.

"How are you, my dear, at all like bloody Jane Eyre?" He laughs, the kind of deep laugh that shows all his lovely teeth, and holds out his glass in my direction. I shake my head. "Jane Eyre is about four feet tall. She's an orphan. She draws crazy brilliant pictures. She has hallucinatory experiences in rooms that are symbolic of menstruation or something. She sort of overreacts a lot. Well, that part is like you." I laugh. Hector knows at least as much about literature as I do, and I never can figure out where he acquires his information. One rarely catches him reading. "You, Janey, are about six feet tall and have a family with a million people in it and cannot even draw a stick-figure dog and are the most sexually appealing woman in the world. Oh yes, and the stupidest one. Because you think you are mousy and invisible. And you are nothing of the sort. Empirically. *Empirically.* Don't you know?"

He has come close to me, and traces his finger, slowly,

up my spine towards the back of my neck. His touch is soft.

"But if you like, you can be Bertha. If it makes you feel better," he says.

IT TURNS OUT THAT THERE ARE Three Horsepersons of the Apocalypse, and I am one of them.

Blanche and Jean and Janet. Horsewomen, I guess. We are programmed to do something next week at the "Symposium on Human Decadence." I had thought it was the two of them doing something and I would supply them with raw data about women's makeovers, but now Jean wants to do an interpretive dance at the opening wine-and-Triscuit reception, and she needs Blanche and me to be her support columns, or book-ends, or something. I am sure this is the end of my academic career, but Jean had a very convincing argument at the time. About how a conference on decadence cannot be the same as every other conference and no one else at the university has the courage to embrace the subject as it ought to be embraced. And if Blanche – quiet, reserved, proper, perfect Blanche – is willing to make a fool of herself, who am I to show the white flag? Granted, Blanche has a one-year contract and not a tenure-track position, and will probably be off in a few months to some other university. Or to Hollywood or something.

In my mind, I see the episode as akin to the embarrassing modernist dance in Ken Russell's *Women in Love,* something with vaguely Greek tunics and goofily waving arms. But Jean has assured me that I can wear something quite ordinary and won't have to move at all.

Jam has arrived. He is staying just two nights, so there is none of the usual laying up of cases of booze. He roughhouses with a delighted Little Max, but is otherwise unusually subdued for Jam. He is acting more like a James. I search my memory for a time when he has ever been like this before, and I cannot recall one. He brushes off my questions about what he wanted to say about Blanche. "Oh that," he says. "Forget about it." The first night he goes to bed before we do. And on Sunday he goes to church with us.

I have only been in church with Jam once before, at our wedding, and I have never been in church with him when he is sober. Hector appears not to notice anything odd about Jam in the least, and is in the high spirits that are usual for him whenever Jam visits. Hector is subbing for our music director today so, once Little Max heads down to Sunday School, I am left alone in the pew with Jam. He fidgets a little and makes fun of the inclusive language of our relatively progressive church. And then he settles down. During the sermon, which is about community, he is strangely still, listening intently. He is looking for something, I think, and I wonder what, if anything, we should say to him.

Little Max brings back a cross made entirely of those little plastic squares that tie up loaves of bread. The glue has been inexpertly applied, and the entire craft soon disintegrates all over the floor. Jam helps me gather up the pieces. Hector supplies a vigorous and somewhat gaudy postlude, and we are released into the September sunshine. We wait on the lawn for Hector to gather up his music.

"Janey, it's your birthday soon, isn't it?" I turn in

mock consternation towards Jam and put my hand on his forehead.

"Jam, Jam, speak to me! Are you okay? Somebody, call an ambulance!" I beckon to Little Max, who is rolling down the hilly lawn of the church property, and is about to smack into a couple of older parishioners with walkers. "Max! Come and help Uncle Jam. He's having a fit. Come and help him." I smile. "Yes, Jam, it's my birthday soon. What are you going to get me? Hector is giving me a gift card to La Vie en Rose, and some colleagues are giving me a makeover. So probably you and Max should go in together and get me Botox injections or teeth whitening or something. No one seems to think I read any more."

"Is that really what Hector is getting you?"

"I don't know. Probably. That's the sort of thing I often get."

"Is that what – is that the sort of thing he would get you when you were still dating?"

I look at Jam sidelong, pretending to be giving most of my attention to Little Max, who is trying to get a beetle to climb up a stick into the pocket of his overalls. "I don't really remember. I don't think fancy lingerie stores existed back then. Why? Are you wondering if you should be buying lingerie for Blanche?"

I am surprised at the response this gets. Jam actually turns, not red, but a pale pink. He is in love. *Is* he in love? "Are you in love, Jam?" Hector comes out and hears this, and hoots.

"How could Jam be in love? There is a bottle of Old Granddad where his heart should be. Let's go to the Pancake House, guys."

We all hate the Pancake House, which is, for some

reason, why we go there. Right after lunch Little Max complains that he feels sick and wants to have a nap, which is so odd that we realize he must truly feel sick, so we go home. Hector drives Jam on some errands to return some borrowed instruments, and I sit with Max in the rocking chair in his room for most of the afternoon, reading to him. He is acquiescent and quiet, unusually so, so I enjoy it.

I don't enjoy it when he starts throwing up. There is no warning, and it is all over my dress, the rug, the furniture. It seems like it won't stop, but of course it does. And until it does I hold him and pat his back in the way he likes and say, "It's okay, honey. It's okay. I'm here. It's okay." This is the only thing I've ever figured out to say to an ill child. Is it enough? What does it mean?

Finally, he settles down enough that I can change his clothes and lay him on his bed, which is relatively unscathed. Then I head off to the closet for rags and a bucket and clean up his room. As always, I think about the fact that no one tells parents how to do this. It's not in the parenting books that I know of. I don't really know what I'm doing, but one of my guiding principles is lots of hot water. I am always surprised at my fortitude in dealing with unpleasantness, if it is my own child's unpleasantness that I am cleaning up. Then I change my own clothes and come back with a pail for his bedside. And then I sit in the rocking chair beside his bed, and it starts again. Mostly in the pail this time. This happens several times in the next two hours, and I have to change clothes a couple of times, and change his too. Poor fellow. I have time, as I sit there patting his back, singing little scraps of songs, to be grateful that this hasn't happened in the middle of the night.

Max is nearly always sick after midnight, but maybe it will all be done before midnight and we can get some regular sleep.

At seven there is no sign of Hector and Jam, and I am starting to get hungry. After all, I'm not sick. I try to creep away from Little Max a couple of times, thinking he is dozing, but he jerks awake and cries for me, and I go back. He is quiet and easygoing as long as I don't make a move to go away.

When they return at ten to eight, I am hopping mad. I stand in the doorway of Max's room, hissing down the stairs at them, and Hector comes up, looking as if nothing is out of the ordinary. He looks concerned for Max when I explain the situation, but not chagrined about his own absence.

"Where the hell have you been? I could use a little help here."

I am surprised by the tone of my own voice. It sounds harsh. Hector is surprised too, and his face becomes unsmiling and stern.

"For God's sake, Janey. We didn't know the baby was sick."

"I'm starving."

"Okay, okay. Go get something to eat, and I'll sit with him." He heads into the darkened room and Little Max wails.

"No! Mommy!"

"Shit," I say, and hesitate on the top of the stairs.

"Just go," I can hear Hector muttering, and then he starts to sing to Little Max, a French lullabye, and Max is quiet.

I recently have been reading Roald Dahl's experiences as a fighter pilot in World War II. There are lots of sentences in *Going Solo* like this one: "I can remember hearing a mighty *whoosh* as the petrol tank in the port wing exploded, followed almost at once by another mighty *whoosh* as the starboard tank went up in flames." And stuff about being ground-strafed. When I got to a section about a huge crowd of Messerschmitts on a bombing raid, I caught myself yawning. Messerschmitts. So what? At this point in his life had Roald Dahl spent several hours in the company of a vomiting toddler? Surely later he did, but never mind. I head down the stairs and think, oh mister man, mothers could tell you a thing or two about torment. You think you know terror? Misery? My mental histrionics make me feel better.

Jam has gone out again. He probably smelled the Mr. Clean and made the correct assumption and bolted. I make some toast and peanut butter, four pieces, and have some chocolate milk. I think of phoning over to my aunt Elizabeth's for help, but she is seventy and arthritic and has never overtly offered to help with Max. She is our only relative in Winnipeg and we don't really know her all that well. She lived in the Yukon for years and has now retired here. Damn, Janey, I say to myself. You and Hector can manage one sick toddler. I scowl at Jam in my mind. I find him self-indulgent. I find his singleness appalling. No, I find his singleness appealing. I want it for myself. I feel the food begin to circulate in my system. I feel better.

Sitting rocking with Max for so much of the afternoon has prompted some idea in me that is hovering just beyond my reach. It is something I wish I could formulate properly. I have felt it at odd times before. It has a bit to do with the .boredom that we aren't allowed to talk about. It is boring being a mother. But what is bothering me is more than that. It is something about the entire basis of domestic life, about what it really feels like, from top to bottom, to be a wife and mother, about the way that no one can explain the feeling to you ahead of time, and once you are inside it, you are too tired or too overwhelmed to articulate it for yourself. Maybe that is it: that there is a secret about family life that no one has ever spoken of because if you are experiencing it your ability to speak it is, by definition, destroyed by exhaustion, frozen by brain atrophy. It is like the lost chord, in that old song by Sir Arthur Sullivan, in a way. You know that some- where this idea, this knowledge exists, but it will always elude you. And there is no way out, no way to escape from this situation of loss and erasure. That's it. There is some knowledge I have about being a wife and mother that I desperately need to express, at least to myself, but it is always being erased at the very instant that I am trying to grasp it or recover it.

Even as I work through this it is slipping away. And all I have is the framework of the notion, in any case. The reality of the notion itself is still ephemeral. If I reached out to grasp it, its outline would dissipate faster. So I sit and play with the crusts of my toast and watch the idea fade slowly. The idea that is not an idea, because I cannot hold it in my head for long enough to trap it, envelop it in language.

I feel smelly and tired but somehow terribly awake. Hector comes down and encases me in his arms. "He's sleeping now," he says. "I'm sorry. Jam is bothered by some stuff, and he wanted to talk, so we went to the

Neighbourhood Café, and I listened to him. I didn't realize how late it was. You shouldn't have had to deal with that yourself."

"I shouldn't have lashed out at you like that," I say. "I was hungry. I feel better now. He was actually pretty sweet this afternoon. It hasn't been that bad. I like being with him when he's sick. I like being useful to him."

"Where is Jam?" Hector looks around.

THE DECADENT DANCE EVENT IS OFF. I am neither surprised nor disappointed. Jean Smothers has pluck, but this seemed beyond even her. But the main thing is that Blanche has disappeared. Well, not disappeared exactly. But she is gone. When I get to the university Monday morning, everyone seems to know that she has gone away unexpectedly, and people are already beginning to speculate about a leave of absence, although term has barely started. But no one really knows. She is out of town, dealing with some kind of crisis in her family. That's the official word.

I am not entirely sure what either Blanche or I were supposed to be doing in Jean's dance, but I am glad that it is moving back into the realm of speculation. Tom has also quit insisting on schemes for guerrilla action at the decadence conference. Once the conference dates came close and the thing became more real, we all found it less funny. As for our feminist dance thing, I assume that Jean no longer needs my makeover research and I tell her that.

"Oh no, Janey. That was a serious present. It wasn't

just for the decadence conference. You have to go. It will be fun. It will do you a world of good."

Do I look like I need to go to a spa? I head to the faculty bathroom later in the morning and examine myself in the mirror. There is a little bit of margarine on my bangs, which must have been there for hours, but other than that I look the same as usual. I think. There is a funny shadow on my chin that is probably a huge blemish coming on. I have curled my hair this morning, but all the curl has fallen out, and my hair sort of hangs there, looking uncared for. I actually did something with my hair, but it undid itself.

My appointment at Giselle's Goddess Aesthetics Chalet is at four thirty. Hector has been at home with Max this morning, and I am to go home and do an afternoon shift, after my eleven thirty class is over. At four, René will stop by to sit with Max until Hector gets home. I have no real idea of how long I will be under the hands of Giselle and company. Suddenly the last thing in the world I want is to be handled by a bunch of shiny, sleek women with advice about my pores. I head out of the bathroom to my office, and suddenly, there is Hector, in the hallway outside my office.

"Honey. Hey. Max was so full of beans that I took him to daycare about a half hour ago anyway. So you don't have to go home this afternoon. He's clearly all right again." Hector looks at my face, and then follows me into my office. "What's the matter?"

"Nothing, really. I can't believe I'm letting any of this stuff bother me. I was worried about the decadent dance, and about the spa thing. I actually feel horrified about the spa appointment. I'm going to cancel it."

Hector contemplates me. "How about if I come too?" he finally says. "And I won't just watch. I'll get a manicure. And a man facial, or whatever they have. And we can be together."

"You have choir, Hector."

"It doesn't start until next week. René will pick up the baby and take him. I've already sorted that."

So this is how Hector and I end up at Giselle's Goddess Aesthetics Chalet together. I tell myself it is just another kind of vanity to get caught up in an anti-vanity tirade, and I should relax and have fun. Hector has a manicure while I have a pedicure, because I have already had a manicure, and we sit side by side, companionably not talking. Then, while we are drinking special and rather unpleasant herbal teas that allegedly are cleaning out our unwanted blood metals or something, we talk about Patient Griselda. The name Giselle reminds Hector of the name Griselda, and he has been thinking about doing a short opera about the tale, and he wants me to do the libretto. I have been teaching Boccaccio's version of the tale, from *The Decameron,* and so it is fresh in my mind. It has possibilities. But there is more material in Chaucer's "Clerk's Tale," and that is the one that Hector is contemplating.

Before I am led away for my facial, we find ourselves laughing over what this aesthetics place would be like if it were run by Patient Griselda. Clients would have to be unceremoniously stripped and taught all sorts of lessons in humiliation. They would be ushered around in rough robes of sacking and told that they were unlovely and useless. And if they didn't bear it patiently and sweetly, Hector says, they would be forced to watch endless episodes of *Baywatch.*

I realize, as I head off to have someone stare at my pores through a magnifying glass, that I have not asked about Jam. Hector was to have taken him to the airport this morning, but I do not know if this has happened. Or what it has to do with Blanche's departure.

OCTOBER

IN-LAWS

APPARENTLY BLANCHE GRIMM IS PREGNANT, AND JAM is THE reason. No one knows this except Hector, who has been sworn to secrecy by Jam. Hector told me, but he knows I will tell no one. Blanche is back teaching, after only five days away somewhere, and she has said nothing about this. Jam is in Ottawa, teaching music at a boys' school and tearing out his hair, this latter detail supplied by Jam himself to Hector. Neither Hector nor I can imagine Jam in such a state, but then again Jam has never been in such a situation. Amazingly.

But it is not really Jam's situation. It is Blanche's. And no one has any idea what is going on with her. Jam told Hector just this week, on the phone, that he has known about the pregnancy for several weeks, and is supposed to keep it quiet for her sake, but he finally broke down and admitted he needed to tell his best friend. Jam used the present tense for the pregnancy. "Are you sure?" I asked Hector afterward. "Why did she disappear and then reappear, ostensibly to get her life started again, if she is still pregnant?" I stared at Hector. "Do you have any idea what Jam is going to do in all this?"

We are still talking about it a week later, in between episodes of *The Odd Couple*. It is Sunday night, and Hector has had a busy weekend of musical events, and old sitcoms help him relax. "I can't see," I say to

Hector, "when they had time to do this. I mean, I know it doesn't take long. But Blanche doesn't seem to be a let's-just-dash-into-this-broom-closet kind of gal. Heavens, they were only together about two or three times, and they were with one of us most of the time. Weren't they?"

I cannot work out the timetable of this. Hector reminds me that Jam spent three weeks on holiday with us, but went off on his own frequently. "I guess he played it close to his chest. Which isn't like him. But still..." Even Hector is a little confused by this, and by Jam's distress. Jam, from a distance anyway, seems to want to take on the challenge of fatherhood, but is having a hard time convincing Blanche that he is serious.

The phone rings. It is Hector's mother. I hand it to him. She never has much to say to me, and I am happy enough with that. She does find time, in the microsecond between hello and asking for Hector, to ask after Little Max, her tone suggesting that the poor fellow must have a hard time getting enough nourishment if I am his mother. I half expect her to ask if he has any clean clothes for school tomorrow. It is all too Dickensian. Do I look like Fagin? Am I sending out Little Max to pick pockets for me? I sigh as I listen to Hector's half of the conversation. Although it is hardly half. It is a small fraction of the airtime. Perhaps eight percent.

"Of course," he says. There is a long pause. "Of course." Another pause. "Yes, we have lots of room. You know that. You'll have our room. We'll bunk in the office. We'll put the cats in the back porch so they don't bother your allergies." Pause. "You know we have cats, Mother." Another long pause. I groan. Hector does not look at me, because, I think, he cannot.

I start a fit of mock weeping, very quietly. "That sounds great." His voice is pleasant but neutral. He does not sound like he normally sounds when he uses the word "great."

Then I hear something different in his voice. "You mean December tenth." It is not a question. It is a statement, and when I hear this tone, one Hector rarely uses, I myself pay attention. But I doubt his mother is alert to such nuance. How Hector, the world's nicest man, was birthed out of this woman is beyond even my considerable imaginative skills. "I thought you said earlier you were coming in the December holidays." Another very long pause, with Hector breathing noisily through his nose and moving the receiver from ear to ear as if were suddenly too hot.

"Of course." He looks at me, finally, and his mouth makes a kissing motion. But his large eyes are serious. "Of course. Well, we're in the middle of term, and both Janey and I are very busy teaching..." He hardly gets out the word "teaching." She has started up again. They don't really believe we have teaching careers. We are just kids. Not doing much. "Well, we'll work it out somehow, and we'll look forward to it. Sure, I'll be at the airport. Goodnight, Mother."

He puts his head in my lap. "I'm so sorry, Janey. I'm so, so sorry."

"What could it possibly be, turnip?" He has requested that I not use any sweet names for him, as he is trying to lose a little weight. He thinks vegetable names will help.

"My parents. I'm sorry that I have parents, Janey. Especially these parents. And I'm super especially sorry that they are coming to stay with us, not in two months, but in three days."

"Three days."

"Three days."

"And I was trying to stop drinking," I say. I try to be sanguine, for Hector's sake. It is harder for him. It really is. I don't like them much, but his mother corners Hector and talks incessantly. She doesn't bother with me, overly. And his father has such a lordly manner. He takes over every space he inhabits, however temporarily. Hector seems rather cowed by him. I think of Charles Van Doren wondering how to deal with the fact that he is Mark Van Doren's son, and thinking he might as well go on a TV quiz show and cheat and make a pile of money and have his reputation ruined forever. These are the sort of issues that Hector might potentially face.

"They told me, ages ago, that they were coming to stay for a week in December, and then going on to the south. But they're spending more of the fall and winter in the south, and they're coming here *now*. She acts as if she always planned it that way. I know that is *not* what she told me." Hector is getting angry now, a rare sight, and he is heading for the liquor cabinet.

I join him there and mix myself a girl drink. Coffee liqueur, diet Coke and skim milk, with lots of ice. I put in a paper umbrella. Hector has a Scotch. I try to give him an umbrella too, to cheer him up, but he absent-mindedly pulls it out and puts it on the windowsill. Where Max will find it tomorrow and stick it in his eye. I retrieve it. He strolls to the piano and picks out a little Mahler ditty, a gloomy one, in the lower octaves. He doesn't say anything, but I stay nearby and we sip our drinks companionably. He is sorting out what to do with his parents, so I let my mind drift back to Jam and

Blanche. What would a child of theirs be like? I cannot begin to imagine, so I move back to the VCR and rewind to the beginning of the *Odd Couple* episode that we had barely started. I start it up again, and look at Hector in a welcoming manner, patting the seat beside me. On the psychedelic blue and purple couch that we really ought to be rid of. But we've had it ever since the beginning of our life together. "Come on, radish. We'll think of something. Maybe we could drug them this time, so they are unconscious for the entire week."

I MET HECTOR FOR THE SECOND TIME on the only occasion I have ever sung in public. It was a charity talent show at a church, raising money for a food bank, and I was singing "Cockeyed Optimist" from *South Pacific* while Tom, whom I knew already, accompanied me (badly) on the harmonica. I was wobbly on the high notes, and not very confident, but was pleased that I was at least getting some volume out *and* remembering the words, when I came to the line about being a dope and full of hope, and I looked out at the little audience, and there was Hector. I wobbled even more, and staggered through to the end. Luckily Tom was so much more unaccomplished than me that my performance looked positively polished by comparison.

I had met Hector the previous night, at a party. We were introduced by someone who was very drunk and who got both our names wrong. So for a few days, as we were starting to see each other, I was under the impression his name was Victor and he thought I was Jeannette. I still have the address book where I wrote his name and number, after the talent show. I got the last name right, Des Roches, but then I wrote "Victor." Sometimes, on anniversary and Valentine's cards I will write: "To my dear Victor. With fond regards, your good friend Jeannette." Or "To Victor, with appreciation for giving me something other than my singing career to think about." Sometimes I think that getting our names wrong did something to bring us together. Sometimes one needs the inauspicious. My singing was certainly inauspicious. I must have been mad to tell him, that first night, that I was singing the next night, and that he should come.

And he did. The next inauspicious thing was that I offered to drive him, about a week later, to an audition and my car, a 1964 Chev, ran out of gas, and he missed the audition completely. The gas gauge never worked on that car. Nothing worked. The wipers worked only occasionally, so if it rained when I was driving I usually found it best to pull over until it stopped raining.

When we decided to get married two years later, we told these stories to the minister who was marrying us and started laughing and laughing, trying hard to get all the details right. "So we sat in the car and talked, and then after a while we went to a nearby Dairy Queen and shared a banana split."

"A Peanut Buster parfait."

"Oh, Hector, I never ate a Peanut Buster parfait in my life."

"Well, maybe I ate most of it."

"And then we caught a bus back to my place, and stayed up all night listening to Sinatra albums, and my cat hated him and scratched him all over his arms, and we didn't get someone to take us back to the Chev for about a week, to fill it with gas."

I remember that the minister made a point, during the wedding homily, of telling about the infectious joy with which we told our stories of meeting. If you ever meet a couple who cannot tell you with pleasure, and in detail, about their meeting, he said, that is a couple in trouble. Possibly an unwise thing for a cleric to say. I remember a few people in the congregation looking uncomfortable. But I mostly remember Hector grinning at me, and his tongue just barely sticking out of the side of his mouth, impishly. What we didn't tell the minister is that we didn't pick up the Chev for a week because we were so fully occupied exploring each other's bodies. Fully clothed, or almost. No coitus. But pretty much the fullest exploration possible under the self-imposed straitened circumstances. I remember it as the most thrilling week of my life.

Lately, Hector has been talking about my singing. I sing at home all the time, and he has been getting me to sing little bits of his Patient Griselda mini-opera so he can hear how the female voice wraps around them. "I like that," he said one night. "Maybe you should sing the part."

"Yeah, cauliflower."

I smile and forget about it almost immediately. When his parents arrive this is, oddly, one of the first things he tells them. Not that I call him cauliflower. But about *Patient Griselda*. "I'm working on a one-act opera, and Janey is going to sing in it." I overhear him say this to his father as they – well, just Hector, really – lift the massive suitcases out of the car. It takes me aback. I did not think the singing thing was at all serious.

"Truly?" says Hector's father, without much interest. He lets Hector carry the bags in, and settles on our screened porch, getting out his pipe. He is a retired music professor from a college even smaller than the one Hector and I teach at, but now that he is settled in his retirement condo in Victoria, somehow his teaching career swells in importance every time we see him. He seems to think Hector's opera is a cute little project. I don't recall that he ever wrote anything except curtain raisers for university functions. I wish I could like him. Like them. Every time I see them, which is not very often, I think that this time it might be a little different. Maybe we will get on better. After all, Hector – *Hector* – is their son.

Hector's mother scampers after him, her high heels slipping and clicking on our old stairs. I wince and wonder if she will tumble. She is seventy-three but cavorts around like she is twenty-three. She is wearing a trim little yellow suit, with a silk blouse and a very tight skirt. I decide Hector has enough on his hands without me trailing behind too, so I scoop Little Max out of their way and urge him gently towards his grandfather.

After a while Emil notices him. "Did you go to school today?"

Max looks at him, then at me, and back at him. "I go to daycare. I'm three. I'm almost four. But I don't go to school, Grandpa. Not yet. I'm only three."

Emil is working away at his pipe, and Little Max is far too interested in the flaming tobacco business for my liking. I try to distract him with a deck of cards that has been left out. He can play a sort of Go Fish, if he concentrates. I hear Emil clear his throat, prior to an announcement.

"Can you play cribbage, Max?"

"Yes." Max always claims to be able to do things of this sort. He has no idea what cribbage is.

"When I was your age, I won a lot of money playing cribbage. I was the best player in town. I taught your father too, when he was your age. He was pretty good. But he didn't keep it up."

"When he was three?" I ask.

"Of course," says Emil, fixing his eyes in a self-consciously pensive manner on a street lamp down the block.

"That seems a little young."

Emil works on his pipe for a while and then turns his eyes again to Max. "Come here."

Max hesitates and I don't blame him. He is a sociable child, but he has not seen his grandparents recently. He knows them, but only just.

"Don't you want to hear what your grandfather wants to tell you?" Emil says and fixes Max in a stare that I know in a Hector version. Hector too has this steady look, but it is much more benevolent.

"No," says Max matter-of-factly. He stands, sturdily, on his own, between us, but keeps me within hailing distance. He stares at his grandfather with a very similar look. Oh boy, I think. Max turns to me. "Can we go to my room and read now?"

I get Emil some iced tea. It is an unseasonably warm evening, a lovely thing, but Emil betrays no pleasure in it. Upstairs, I can hear Mavis's heels clicking on the third floor, back and forth, back and forth. How can one woman walk so much? What the hell is she doing? Max and I go and read *Mop Top* for the millionth time, and *The Cat in the Hat Comes Back*. He likes that one better than *The Cat in the Hat*. I wonder why. Are all the little invisible cats better than boring old Thing One and Thing Two? Well, of course they are. There are twenty-eight agents of mayhem in the sequel and only three in the original. More chaos is better. Max particularly likes the page with the bizarre injunction, bizarre even for Dr. Seuss, to *kill the snow*. I wonder if a children's author would have the temerity to write that now. I have a moment's misgiving as I think of Mavis, up in our room, looking at the poster of our Modigliani nude. It is a tasteful nude, and she has seen it before. But still. I would have taken it down, put up a Monet landscape. But Hector insisted we do no more than change the sheets and sweep the floor. "The woman is supposed to be coming in two months. She is not, in reality, here." He was adamant.

I have a tough time getting Max into the bathtub tonight. He senses tension in the air and decides to work with it. All the time I am supposedly playing with toy boats and frogs, he senses I am not really with him, and I'm not. I'm thinking of how I'm going to get any prep done for my classes this week when Emil and Mavis are here.

My course in the nineteenth-century novel is going okay; I have taught it several times. And first-year Lit is going fine. I could do it in my sleep, and frequently have, or almost. But I am also teaching a new course, in non-fiction, which is giving me trouble, and as I look at texts before I teach them, I wonder why I put them on the syllabus. I have already cancelled a couple of essays that I had previously liked, but now seem to me vapid. I had hoped to teach some of George Orwell's non-fiction, which I think is superior to his fiction, but there is not an entire Orwell book that I like. I like half of *Down and Out in Paris and London* and nearly half of *The Road to Wigan Pier*. But the books themselves don't hold together, and I really don't want the course to turn into one where the students deride and dump on the authors. I want them to admire Orwell for all that was splendid in his character, and make a passing acquaintance with all that was, admittedly, unappealing. He was not always, or perhaps even often, truthful. I need to spend some time this evening making decisions about whether I should cancel a few more of the readings on the syllabus and put replacements on reserve in the library. These students did not much like Woolf's *A Room of One's Own*. How does one reach students like these?

Max senses my lack of interest in tub toys and starts to kick water. I like giving him baths; it is one of the parenting chores that I am pretty good at. But far from perfect. Always, no matter how well our bath session is going, I recall at the back of my mind a terrible evening about eight months ago when I could not get him to co-operate about rinsing his hair, and I had to hold his little head down in the water, swishing the hair back and forth, and he shrieked as if I were drowning him. Briefly, very briefly, the thought had crossed my mind. It was awful, and I wish I could forget it. But Jake would probably say that forgetting is exactly what I ought not to try to do, as it won't work anyway. I am working with Jake on parenting issues now. Better not tell Mavis.

Mavis opens the door as Max is giving a mighty splash, and her turquoise silk blouse gets wet. The bathroom is small. "Oh Max," I say, and smile at Mavis, winningly, I hope. She does not look at either of us, and is dabbing away at her blouse. I heave a tiny sigh and look at Little Max. He meets my eye, and his eye seems to say, "You wanted me to do it." I nod at him. He holds up his arms to be lifted out.

Wrapping him in the towel has to be one of the favourite parts of my day. Did any child ever, wrapped in a towel, not look adorable? I mentally challenge Mavis to look at him, but she is arching her eyebrows and pursing her lips at herself in the mirror. Now she is looking about for a suitable space to put all her sprays and unguents. I forgot about this aspect of having her in my home. How could I forget? At home she has a broad vanity table, with a triptych mirror and special lights, for all her coiffing and bejewelling needs. Last time we went through this. Our room had neither adequate light nor electrical supply for Mavis's liking, so she filled up our lone bathroom with at least a dozen bottles and several appliances. She made Hector drag in a special little table for her equipment and install extra wattage, which nearly killed me when I had to go in there in the deadly pre-coffee time in the mornings.

"So," says Mavis, without looking at either me or Little Max, "are you trying to do something a little different with your hair?"

"I don't know," I say. And I don't. "I hadn't really thought about it." I hesitate. Will this bring us closer together, if I ask her for advice? "What do you think I should do with it?"

She swings around, girlish and energetic. Yes, this was the right move, but I'll have to be careful or I'll get cornered in the kitchen some evening with tinfoil wrapped around various sections of my head. Mavis reaches out and paws at my hair. Max wiggles free from us and dashes off down the hall, loving his own nakedness. I look at him, long to be naked too.

"What about some colour, Janet? Have you thought about what colour you might like?" Mavis's own colour is gold, a strange gold that seems like late sixties or early seventies sofa cushions. A rec room colour.

"I wouldn't mind having black hair," I say, not very seriously. I stand behind Mavis and we look at each other in the bathroom mirror. I am much taller than she is. I have to stoop to look into my own mirror. I lived in this house five years before I realized I was stooping to look into the mirror. Mavis would have noticed that instantly and had someone rectify it. And installed a row of globular dressing-room lights, each with one hundred watts of pure firepower. I have been in her bathroom and counted the watts: six hundred of them. Agony. I had to wear sunglasses to go in and pee one morning, early in our marriage, when we'd been out for drinks the night before with some of Hector's high school friends. That's more wattage than on most Broadway marquees.

"Oh, dear, no, not black. Terrible for your particular complexion." I'm surprised she didn't say "peculiar." I think she wanted to. There are days when there is, I think, a greenish tinge to my face, but that's if I've had trouble sleeping or Little Max has kept us up. "What about a kind of rosy auburn colour?"

I squint at myself in the mirror. I imagine something sort of pumpkin-y happening around my head. "Hmmm. I don't quite see it, Mavis. Oooh, I'd better get Max in his pyjamas." I knew from the first time I met Hector's mother that I would be a disappointment as a daughter-in-law. Hector is an only child, and Mavis clearly wanted a big dress-up girl doll to play with. And I wasn't very cooperative. In the early years she would buy me silver and gold sweaters, always too small for my long body, and large, chunky necklaces. Later this stopped, when she realized that she never saw them on me. I would have worn them, if I could, to keep the peace, but I couldn't. And the necklaces, without fail, have looked ludicrous.

Later, in the spare bed in the office, Hector and I lie there, giggling like kids at summer camp, doing imitations of his father. We don't mock Mavis, for some reason, probably because she is the more dangerous of the two. I take her quite seriously as a combatant. But Emil is fair game. Hector does a passable imitation of Emil's noble stare off into the middle distance, drawing on his pipe and saying, "Truly? Truly? Yes, well, mmm, I had a similar experience in my time at Canterbury." He went there once, for a week, for a conference, but you'd think he was just under the archbishop the way he says it. Emil also likes to pretend that his faith has led him to experience a life of prejudice and difficulty. The Des Roches family is officially Roman Catholic, although Hector says that worship was never a regular thing when he was growing up. When Hector and I first took them to our liberal Protestant congregation, Emil dropped many dark hints about consorting with the adversary, about ethical compromise and settling for less. If anyone else had done this, I would have been insulted, but I've been trying to avoid being insulted by the Des Rocheses for years.

"He claims that both he and you picked up cribbage

at Max's age. At three or four."

"Oh, that could well be true for him," says Hector, loyally. "He really was some sort of prodigy with numbers. But not me. I had trouble counting even in kindergarten. I remember my mother getting quite perturbed..."

Overhead, we have been hearing the steady murmur of Mavis's voice, with very occasional punctuation by Emil. Suddenly, both of their voices break out, loudly and fiercely. Hector and I stare up at the ceiling, paralysed.

We can only make out segments of the argument.

"How could you, how dare you –"

"...never said anything of the..."

"And then, to have the temerity to say –"

"Oh stop it. Why do you –"

It is gruesome. When I first heard one of these, years ago, Hector was mildly embarrassed and apologetic, but we are long past this stage. We sigh together, two kids trapped in the back seat of the car with two adults arguing about who left the map back at the hotel room. As the signpost for the turnoff that is wanted goes past, unheeded by any except us. The main thing I feel these days, whenever Mavis and Emil go through town on their way somewhere, is how dreadful it must be to be together on these Mexican or Florida holidays, stuck together for months with only this person who drives you crazy for companionship.

"Oh, no, it doesn't work like that," says Hector. "She immediately takes up with people and golfs and plays tennis a lot, and he pretends to learn new scores. But really he just naps a lot and smokes and reads all the papers. They aren't forced together that much.

They find it harder at home, really. They fought a lot more when I was a kid."

"I don't get it," I say, and find a place for my head near the hollow of his neck. "How did you turn out so swell? You are so peaceful. Most of the time. Anyway, you are very peaceful to me."

"Well, that is because I have a hidden and dastardly motive with you, Janey. I never know when I might want you to satisfy me, so I have to stay on your good side. Like now, maybe." I curve my body, appreciatively, beside him. "Anyway," says Hector, "don't you think if you had parents who fought like that, you might want to try something different? That's what my goal was."

"Admirable," I say. "Most people would end up mimicking their terrible families."

"Oh, they're not terrible, are they? It's just that she should have done something more. She's the last of that generation of women trained to run a household, and not much else. She has great organizational skills and nothing much to organize. Only one kid. She could have been a bank manager or something. But she was taught how to get stains out of everything, and how long you have to wait between perms."

The noise upstairs is escalating and ends in a short shriek from Mavis. I turn in alarm towards Hector, but he is already smiling at me reassuringly. "No, it's okay. It's her benediction. It's over now."

At breakfast, the two of them are serene and fit-looking. I never can see how people look like that in the morning. I trail around in my favourite long black nightgown, with a shawl and long warm socks. I have tried to smooth down my hair, but I like to drink my coffee horizontal, on the couch, alone; I think I fool with my hair as I do it, waking up gradually, watching the play of the sunlight through the elms and through the bevelled glass in our front windows. Today, I cannot lie on the couch. There are too many witnesses, and I have to be upright, which bores me. I might as well go have a shower.

Hector grabs me in the hallway and pulls me into the office, which now looks like the hotel room of a college football squad on the road. "While they're here," he says quietly, "they might as well be useful. They can stay with Little Max one of these nights, and we'll go out for dinner."

"I thought we'd have René in, and we would take *them* out for dinner."

"I thought so too, but they forfeited their right to our company by that repellent display of bad manners last night." I nod in agreement. "The only downside to going out without them is we can't make them pay if they're not along. Too bad." Hector looks at me. "We're up awfully early. I don't teach until ten, and Little Max will surely sleep until at least eight thirty." He manoeuvres me towards the Hide-A-Bed. "How about it? I knew there was a reason we never made the bed this morning."

"But we never do make our bed, Hector."

"I've noticed that about you. You minx. You are always scheming to get me back in there."

"I haven't brushed my teeth."

"Yeah? I care?" And he settles enough of his weight on me that it crushes the fretfulness out of my body, leaving only him. And me.

IT IS TOM WHO COMES TO OUR RESCUE with the in-laws. Tom is marginally involved with an oral history conference at the other university, and it turns out that both Mavis and Emil know some doddering retirees writing about the prairies. So Tom escorts them to two days worth of presentations and muffin snarfing, and we can actually keep to our regular teaching and mark-ing schedules, sort of. But I find, in my office one afternoon, that I am not marking or making teaching notes, but roughing out the plot for a murder mystery.

It becomes addictive. I email it to myself at home, and after Max is in bed that night, I open up the file and keep working at it. It seems like it might have a sort of *Thin Man* tone, updated, with a smart-ass husband and wife who solve mysteries on the side. On the side of what? In my outline, I scribble various possi-bilities. They are realtors. There are probably not enough realtors in literature, but I am hampered by the fact that I know nothing about real estate. They are screenwriters. I see her as a Dorothy Parker character, so this works fairly well, and the movie background would bring glamour and lots of piquant crime possibil-ities. But surely the intersection of Hollywood and crime has been overcrowded for years. What about inventors? That would be cool, but again, what do I know about invention? They would surely be rather practical people, in a way, and I am not very practical. I leave them as lit-erature professors for now, as a temporary placeholder.

Now, victims, that is where the interest is. Not so much in the criminal. I don't believe in valorizing evil-doers too much, so I don't want to create perversely attractive murderers. But victims, that's what will make my murder mysteries stand out. I am working on this outline, noting down ideas and names and plot points in a random way for about an hour, when Hector pokes his head in.

"Quit it. Stop working. Stop right now."

"I'm not working," I say. "I don't think I'm working. It doesn't feel like that. I think I'm writing a mystery."

"You are not. You're working. Stop it. Come down here and help me ask them to look after Max tomorrow night. They're gone soon, and this will be the last chance." I don't want to be part of this appeal and think it would come better from Hector alone, but I see that he wants me along, so I move my chair back and get up and follow him. I am reluctant to move away from the mystery idea. I haven't felt this at home with a project, this comfortable, since my MA thesis. I did an edition of some Kingsley Amis juvenilia, which was fairly lightweight and was never published. But the project was a good fit for me, in a way that my PhD work, a more straightforward evaluation and analysis of a grouping of sixties British novels involving religion, never was.

"Will it make us rich?"

"What?"

"Your mystery novel."

"What do you want to be rich for?"

"So we can get a nanny and go to Fiji every winter. And be naked every day."

"I'll do my best."

We walk out onto the screened porch, where we have placed a couple of lights for Hector's father to read his paper in the autumn evenings, while he smokes his pipe. Mavis is doing her nails and reading *People* at the other end of the porch. I hear a thump and a screech from the back of the house. Poor Helen and Adele have been shut up for most of this week, and although they have access to the basement, as well as the back porch, they are getting understandably restless.

I sit down close to Mavis. This is what is expected of me. I am nearly always drawn to men and find their company more congenial. But I am a daughter-in-law and there are expectations. Mavis looks at my dress, a kind of brown tunic over dark leggings. "Do you want me to work on that grease stain this evening?" I look down. I had not known there was a grease stain. Suddenly I am filled with something. Not rage, exactly, although that is close. I am glad they have to go soon. I hope it is awhile before they come back. She has replaced all our dish towels this week, declaring our old ones to be rags. She took Little Max for a haircut without consulting anyone. It is terribly short, and he looks like a kid in a Dick and Jane reader. She keeps tidying his hair with a wet comb, making a sharp part. He doesn't look like himself. Emil has asked Hector rather pointed questions about his salary and his savings that make me uncomfortable. For one thing, it was *his* savings that Emil asked about, not *ours*. As if a divorce were imminent. And when the rice I made last night refused to become rice, mysteriously, and became crunchy white mush, Mavis shooed us out of the kitchen and made a complicated noodle dish that was fairly quick and tasted great, but involved a lot of pots and dishes that Hector and I had to offer to wash afterward. Something is rising in my chest, and I know exactly what the victim in my murder mystery will look like, her voice, her mannerisms. I can even hear the sound of her little heels clicking to her certain doom.

NOVEMBER

IN LOVE

WHAT HAPPENS WHEN YOU ARE VERY MUCH IN LOVE with your husband, but you have erotic dreams about nearly anyone and everyone else? I ponder whether I should ask Jake this, or Hector himself. Sometimes I tell Hector my erotic dreams, as he is never jealous and always stirred up by them. But lately they come in such profusion that even Hector must start to have misgivings about my loyalty. What is going on?

There is one student, a clever young man, who features in a lot of my dreams. In my waking hours I don't even like him that much. He has an attitude to go with his intelligence, and seems to take my courses on sufferance. He is not even as tall as I am, and I am not conscious that I am attracted to him. But there he is in my dreams. When he comes into my office with a question or a form to sign, I jump guiltily. I feel transparent around him, unprofessional. I also feel like I'm about sixteen. I thought, when I was full of rampaging hormones as a teen, that people in their forties were dried up and ancient, past desire. Surely they never had racy dreams. But here I am, and they're getting racier.

I am on the bus, on the way to campus. Hector has taken the car earlier, to a meeting, and dropped Little Max off at daycare. I've noticed an improvement in the time it takes to get Max ready for daycare in the mornings. There are still struggles, but not nearly so many. He's eating a little less fussily. Since I worked with Jake on my old anxiety, I am, apparently, easier to be with. I can see it, myself, in the way Max is relating to me. He still pounds on the piano when I am on the phone, but less often.

I am not trying to review the latest dream, but it unfolds before me anyway, even though I have *Mrs. Dalloway* open on my knee. In the dream I am a graceful forest animal, a deer or a gazelle, and I am being pursued in the forest by other animals, and by human hunters. But then I am not an animal, but myself when younger, and I am doing one of those trying-to-run-but-can't things. "Oh-ho, you want to get caught," says a voice. It is something that Hector says to me, but I look over my shoulder, and it is him. The other him. This student. And there are lots of people watching. Tom. Hector's parents. Beatrice. Burton Cummings. The dream then moves to a firehall, and there's a lot of sliding down poles and bells ringing and, at one point, a Highland dance competition and a brief liaison with Antonio Banderas. Not my type at all. And it goes on from there.

I am at my stop, and I see Blanche crossing the street towards our university building. I hurry to catch up with her. She has been away at a conference in the States, and I ask her how her paper went. Fine, she says, and she turns her dark eyes on me.

"Oh, Janey," she says suddenly, and she is crying, her face buried in my shoulder. She has never called me Janey before, and I have never had to comfort a weeping colleague in the front courtyard before ten a.m. I try to think where to steer her. We head for the faculty washroom and lock the door. I find her some Kleenexes.

"I'm sorry," she says. Her weeping has made her

look more like a human being and less like a goddess. Her face is like mine; it gets streaky and blotchy. Her nose is bright red. "I don't know how much you know about this."

"A little," I admit. "Jam and Hector are very close. And Hector tells me everything."

"I talked to Jam on the phone a few nights ago," she says. "He was so upset with me. So upset." There is a silence. I wait for her to explain.

"Did you know I was pregnant?" I nod and make note of the past tense this time. Oh dear. Poor Blanche. Poor Jam. "It's hard, you know? Hard to decide." I nod again. "It was so much harder to decide than I ever thought it would be. I'm a practical person. I'm an independent person. I live alone. I don't really have a home. I'm not ready to settle yet. I have research and things I want to do in lots of places..." She has collapsed onto an old wooden chair in the corner of the bathroom. She has not looked in the mirror and tried to fix her face so she can rush out and resume her day. I admire that.

"And I hardly know Jam. And something like this. A pregnancy when you've known someone a few days. It's ridiculous, right? But I thought hard about it. And talked to him a lot, on the phone. And I felt like I got to know him really well, over the past little while. And we're so comfortable together." She blows her nose. "Well, we were."

She stands up now. "Once I made my decision, it wasn't so comfortable. He was so hurt. I thought he would understand. I think he does understand. But, well, it's so emotional." She says this with some wonder, as if emotion is something rather new in her life. Oh baby, I think, let me tell you some stories.

"I went ahead and had the abortion. I didn't have it here in the city. I went home, and stayed with my parents. I did go to the conference, but left right after my session and flew home." She looks at me. "I thought I would feel okay, feel better by now. But I don't. I feel – terrible."

"I know," I say. And I do.

"The political beliefs, they're...they're fine, in their place. But this doesn't feel very political at all just now." She hesitates, looks into my face, searchingly. "When will it start to feel better?"

I sigh. "Oh, it will take quite a while." She shakes her head, closes her eyes and reaches out both her hands for mine. I stand beside her in the corner of the bathroom, holding her hands, awkwardly. But it feels good. I don't care where I have to be this morning. This is life and death. It really is. How often are our days really about life and death?

"You should go home. What are your classes today?"

"Just Intro Women's Studies."

"What are you doing?"

"*A Room of One's Own.*"

"Hey, Blanche, that is the one Women's Studies text I can do. I'll take it, and do something or other. I'll try not to ruin them for you. You go home. Okay? You really ought to. And would you like it if – if I came over tonight, and spent the evening with you?"

We agree to this. "Have you talked to Jam in the last couple of days?" I ask.

She shakes her head. "I spoke to him three nights ago for the last time. He said, he said...that he was not going to be speaking with me again."

"Oh. Oh, honey."

"Thank you, Janey." She smiles at me, painfully. "You're wonderful. You really are. Do you know that?"

"No. Not really," I say. "It's nice to hear it."

INTRODUCTION TO WOMEN'S STUDIES is a big class, about seventy-five students, and seventy-three of them are women. A room with this many women makes me nervous. As I look out at them I find it hard to think of them as women. Surely these do still qualify as girls. Can I say that, even to myself? Most of them aren't more than eighteen. There are a few older women scattered through the lecture hall, but there are definitely a lot of girls.

They all have their slim, shiny, apparently unopened copies of *A Room of One's Own* sitting on their desks. The way I teach works better if the students have actually read the book. I teach informally, with a lot of open-ended questions and areas of rambling discovery. But I need someone to discover it with me. If it's just me standing up there doing the rambling and discovering, the whole enterprise starts to resemble a dentist working on a mouth that has no teeth. It becomes surreal.

I ask them, bluntly, if they've read it. I find it hard to be this frank, even this rough, with my own students. But these aren't mine, which is liberating. Maybe they need someone to shake them up a little. "How many people," I say, at the start, before I've even told them who I am or where Blanche is, "have actually read this book?"

About ten students put up their hands. Not enough. I consider chasing the whole gang out of the room. After all, it is a very short book. "This is a very short book," I say. I glare at them, as best I can. Probably I look constipated. I look at my notes on *Room,* then up at them again. About four of these students are also in my non-fiction class, I can see, so they've already heard my spiel on Woolf's great feminist essay. I need something new. I hate it when students have to hear me repeat stuff I've already done.

I'm thinking fast, on my feet, which does not come easily to me. First, I read them the bit about Woolf wanting to pave the way for women to have freedom to enter more professions in one hundred years. "And really, it didn't take that long. This project has already been a success, in much less time. Hasn't it?"

I wait for a response. Not surprisingly, there isn't one. I wait more. I've been around. I know the value of letting the silence linger a little longer.

"Well, yes," says a girl I know who sometimes comes to our peace group. "Look at this classroom. This would have been impossible to imagine, a few years ago."

"I wonder," I say. "Who was the audience for Woolf's talk?" One of the older students knows; after all, it's there at the front of the book. "Right. She gave a series of talks to women students in two women's colleges in Cambridge in 1928. What do you – all of you – look like right now?" I sweep my arm around the room. "Look at each other."

They do. It is a room heaving with perky breasts. "Is this really all that different? Sorry, guys." I look at the two guys at the back, whose faces are impassive. There is another one in the front, at ease with women of all stripes. He has multiple piercings and longish hair with a chunk of purple colouring in it. He looks very comfortable with his sexualities, which are probably multifarious and interesting. He is wearing a Hello Kitty T-shirt.

"What would Virginia Woolf think about Women's Studies programs in universities?" I pick out a clever student I know from my own class. I know she's read the book. "Hailey. What do you suppose?"

"She would have been pleased. And proud." Hailey taps her pencil on the desk. "She wanted women to know that women, as a subject of contemplation, as a subject of discourse, were worth it."

"Yes," I say, "but..." And then one of the other young women who has read the book breaks out over top of me.

"But," she says, "what is all that section about the feminine and the masculine way of writing about, if she's so thrilled about women's studies? She says there's a masculine sentence and a feminine sentence, and then she goes on to hope for something else, an androgynous sentence."

"Yes." I say this more definitively. We can talk this over for a while, even with those who haven't read the book. And then I ask them about how Woolf's sense of humour works, what they notice about it. I read sections to them that I find very funny. They don't seem to find them as funny as I do, but still the students work with me, trying to answer my questions. We talk about her emphasis on food. "Why does she go on about the prunes, and the port, and all that?" None of them had thought about Woolf as a political person, beyond her obvious feminism. "Food is economics. Especially, at the time, perhaps even still in our time, for women. Food is the one part of the household economy that a woman of that time definitely had to understand and grasp. Even if she was an upper middle class woman, with servants, like Virginia Woolf."

The class is nearly over, and it has gone okay. I ask them to think about a few things and bring them to Blanche next time. "We've talked about professions that have opened to women since Woolf's day: law, medicine, university teaching. But I'd like you to find out how many women orchestra conductors there are in North America today. And bring to next class the names of as many women classical composers as you can. Find out how many women are in Wynton Marsalis's Lincoln Center Jazz Orchestra. And finally, find out how many female students placed in the top one hundred in the provincial grade twelve mathematics tests last year."

I let them go and hurry down the hall to my own class. Intro Lit. We are doing *Mrs. Dalloway,* so it feels as if there is a neat synchronicity. I head into the room, and it is buzzing with conversation. I like the noise. Blanche's class had three times as many people, but was nearly silent on my entry. My students are in an uproar about something.

"Dr. Janey. Did you hear about this?" Jee-Anne, my peace group comrade, in her final year, is waving the student newspaper around. She is a conflict resolution student and never got around to taking English until I talked her into it this year. "Student council – those fascists! – are cutting off funding to the women's centre."

Several English students are active on the student paper and several more are on student council, so there are lots of opinions in the room. I wondered why the Women's Studies class was not abuzz with this issue. "What's it about?" I say.

A student named Nick explains. "This guy, Dennis Sailor – you remember him, Dr. Janey – he ran for student council president last year, and lost. He put himself forward as a member of the board of directors of the women's centre. And they wouldn't let him, of course, and he got his cronies on student council to vote to withdraw funds from the women's centre. And then him and his Christian group, last night, they started papering the windows of the women's centre with pictures of fetuses and stuff..."

"Really?" I murmur, and then, through our open door, we hear the crash of glass. We go silent for a second. And then the kids are talking excitedly and some of them move towards the door. "Whoa," I say. "I'll go, and..." I look around. "You, Jeremy, will you come with me, and Rachel too, and we'll find out what's going on? The rest of you, stay put."

I smile calmly. I am good in a tricky situation. I always have been. "So much for my trying to figure out how to tie this discussion to *Mrs. Dalloway*," I say to the two of them. "It could have been done, quite easily." And it could have.

We round a corner into the central section of the university's main building. The women's centre is down below, and that's where the hubbub is. Looking down over the railings, I can see that someone has thrown something and smashed the glass window of the women's centre, and there is a short, fiery red-headed woman yelling ferociously at a couple of other women, and a crowd of students trying to be peacemakers. Rachel and Jeremy and I watch for a moment, and then I say, "I think we would just be a nuisance, don't you?" and we head back to give our report. The university president is down there, I can see, and she's a smart cookie, and the custodians and security guards are there too.

Too much synchronicity, I think. I'm glad Blanche is off campus today.

MY ELECTRONIC CROSS-BORDER literary journal is going nowhere. There was a committee formed in August to try to draft a short statement of purpose, and they are stuck. I am leaving them alone, because I don't want the very first task on this journal to end up back on my desk, with me doing it alone. That doesn't bode well. I'm trying to learn how to be more collegial and I'll never get anywhere if I take things over and do them all myself, in my half-assed way. Anyway, I am more interested in my murder mystery these days.

To kill off one's mother-in-law in a novel is too trite and makes me uneasy. So I am busy trying to disguise Mavis. She is not a mother to anyone in the book, but is a Tory politician. This is a real part of Mavis's personality, so it isn't that hard to work with this version of her. When we first met, I had an unpleasant conversation with her about women's rights, about abortion and contraception. I found her particularly obtuse on the issue of women's shelters. "Shelters from what?" she demanded. "From husbands? From the husbands they have promised to support?"

"I think they cease to be husbands as soon as they start beating their wives."

"Oh, beating. People use that word as if they knew what it meant. Often what they really mean is a little tap on the behind. When I was growing up, we kept our family problems in the family. And we solved them in the family."

I ended up, that time, saying as calmly as I could that I didn't think we should talk about this subject any more and removing myself as gracefully as I could. I was careful never to talk politics with Mavis again, although she would continue to throw out remarks that begged to be challenged. "Do you see that Indian woman over there? What is she doing out with a baby stroller at ten thirty at night?" I would answer Mavis silently in my head. Maybe this is the best and safest place for her baby and her right now. I had a difficult time not losing my temper when I found out that she was proposing the name Chastity for our baby if the baby was a girl. We had not canvassed them for their opinions, but opinions were offered anyway. Chastity, according to Mavis, is one of the prime virtues. She has never known that if Max was a girl I wanted to name her Pax. She kicked up a fuss when I took Max, as a six-week-old baby, on a peace march. She had been staying with us, to help with laundry and such, and Hector sent her home shortly thereafter. I found the way she folded his underpants unnerving.

How to kill my politician victim? Something fairly straightforward, I think. A whack across the head. I don't know anything about ballistics or poisons. And really, isn't a whack across the head quite hard to solve? I would think so. No complicated instruments are needed. Any ordinary room has a dozen weapons to hand. Yes, I'll whack her across the head with a marble bookend in a living room. And it can be wiped and put back in place, holding up all those dusty Britannicas, and the clever detective couple will crack the case merely by noticing that the line of dust has shifted a bit on the encyclopedia. Hmmm. I've sorted the whole thing out too quickly. Anyway, I will build in a whole lot of characters for colour and delightful mystification.

I do notes for the novel for half an hour until supper, and then get up and put on some water for spaghetti as Max and Hector come through the door. I kiss them both, and Max runs off to the cookie jar. It is a mistake, but I let him, so I can kiss Hector some more. "How long have we been married?" I ask him.

He thinks. "Eleven years?"

"Oh, Hector. This is going to be thirteen. Don't you remember?"

"I don't remember the number. I remember the experiences. Especially the ones involving that jumpsuit you used to have. Where is that tight jumpsuit, Janey? You know the one."

"Be serious," I say. "Are we happy?"

"I refuse to answer that dumb question," he says, and opens up the can of spaghetti sauce. "Max, do you have to go to the bathroom?"

The phone rings, and we ignore it. The cats are prowling, because there are meatballs. "Okay, so we're happy," I say. "Don't you wish that Jam had a life at least a little like ours? Or can't you imagine it for him?"

"Sure, I can," says Hector. "Max, I think you do

need to go to the bathroom. Do you want Daddy to involves – I don't know – joy and unconditional mutual adoration and stuff. And cocktails and sex. And great literary discussions. And peeing. Who wouldn't want that for his best friend?"

I tell Hector about my morning encounter with Blanche. He shakes his head and sits down. "Damn, that's hard. For both of them. I guess I thought that this is what would happen, but they weren't saying anything. And you sorta hope that maybe they'll figure out what to do together somehow." He paused. "But it looks like this will drive them back to their separate lives. They were both pretty solitary people before. Really. Jam is a party boy, but he's been alone, really, for a long time. Can you write Parmesan cheese on the list?"

I scoop a cat, Adele, off the counter and shoo her into the back porch and close the door. I hear a protesting yowl. "I'm going over to Blanche's tonight. Thought I'd sit with her and see if she wants to talk. Or just sit. Or something. Is that okay?" Hector nods. I cut up cucumbers and he puts Little Max's spaghetti in the freezer for a moment. We move together, completing the several steps to make Max's hot chocolate so it is just the way he likes it.

I HAD AN EMAIL THIS WEEK from a journal to which I had sent a piece on Iris Murdoch. It has been rejected. They don't seem to want to see a revision, although their note is worded more ambiguously than usual. I will give up on this essay now. This is the third time it's been turned down by a journal, and every time the reasons given have been quite different. I am discouraged, and at the same time I don't give a damn. But I know this latter feeling is a dangerous one. Once I stop caring, depression can lurk, and it is only November. I cannot get depressed in November. I don't have time.

Our anniversary is coming up, and the actual date is an awkward fit, so on a Friday evening we book René to stay overnight for the first time and drive about two kilometres from our house and check into a hotel. We make love right away and then lie in bed talking. I find I'm back in Brontë territory again, talking about the way women are drawn to bad men. Hector listens for a while, his eyes half closed.

"I am not Rochester, you know," he says after a bit.

"I know. You said that."

"But I'm really not. I'm not a bad man. You'll have to accept that, Dr. Janey."

I wonder if this is what is behind my erotic dreams of late. That I seem to long for someone who is bad for me because my own husband is too nice. I note that I dream of a student I don't even like, someone I think may even be antagonistic towards me. I don't say any of this, but lie there, stroking Hector's arm and shoulder. The room is warm and I am starting to fall asleep. I feel as if we are somehow melting into each other. No, really it feels as if we are cooking together, being cooked. We are savoury together. We are a delicious meal.

I am falling asleep. I raise myself on my arm and look at the clock. It is seven thirty in the evening. We've only been here since six. Hector is asleep. I grin at him. His hair is long again, over his forehead at least, and it has fallen over his eyes. I reach over and turn out the light, and we sleep until five the next morning, when we wake up, make love again, have a shower together and then go sit at Starbucks and drink strong coffee and read trashy fiction until it is time to go home to Max at eleven. René has a guitar lesson.

Later, we will probably wonder what we did on this little anniversary jaunt, but it feels like the most satisfying holiday I've ever had. When we get home, René says that Jam has called three times. Hector calls him back.

Jam is quitting his boys' school job, which was only half time anyway. It is part-way through term but he doesn't care. He has some savings he can live on for a while, because he has always lived cheaply, sharing houses and house-sitting. He's coming here. He doesn't mention Blanche's name, but, as Hector tells it, she was clearly underlying the entire conversation. Hector said he could stay with us, and then they talked about a whole bunch of church music jobs that Jam could easily walk into at short notice. According to Hector, church gigs are easy to come by and good money. Jam can play almost any instrument.

I wish I had talked to Jam. I wish I could have heard the tone of his voice, to gauge how to feel about this, for Blanche's sake. That evening I spent with her was a little heartbreaking. She is a strong person, but anyone would feel vulnerable at such a time, and she was having a tough time with that vulnerability. She seems, in some respects, a terrible match for Jam. And in other ways, a good one, a challenging one. I think maybe she's in love with him. But I don't know. It's not our call. Probably no one who knew Hector or me separately would ever have been able to predict the way we came together and what our marriage is now like. I don't know if I could explain it myself.

After René leaves, Max climbs up on my knee and gives me a tight hug. Hector is on the phone still. Max gives an experimental tug on my earring, and then a harder one. "Hey," I say. "No thank you." I move him to one side and stand up and transfer myself to the window seat across the room. Max comes and stands beside me, drumming on my thigh with a board book he wants me to read to him. I look out the window.

"Do you know what I want for my birthday?" he asks. I sigh. He has been talking about his birthday for ages, and it always escalates, involving ever more expensive gifts and complex themes. The last one was *Star Wars* and involved a piñata for every guest. And he wanted to invite about fifteen kids. It is coming up in a few weeks. We will have to make a decision soon. "One piñata. Shaped like a sun. I saw it at the drugstore," he says. "That's all."

I give him, belatedly, the whole of my attention. "That's all?"

"That's all."

I open my arms and he climbs back up on my lap. We look at the dog across the street, which has an owner patient enough to play fetch with it for about an hour a day. I couldn't do it. "Do you know what Gayle says?" Gayle is one of Little Max's daycare workers. "She says I have transition issues."

"Transition issues," I say. I try to keep the amazement out of my voice. Admittedly Max has said "tralls-ition," but I can follow. He seems to know what he's saying.

"Gayle says it's hard. For me. To switch from one

activoli to another." I hesitate and then nod. *Activity.* Yes.

"Gayle is very smart," I say. "That sounds accurate to me. Does Gayle say what we can do about these transition issues?"

"She didn't really say," says Little Max. "But she gave me a notebook. And it's my journal. And she's putting in a schedule – in it for me. And I will write how I feel about it."

I ask him to get the notebook, which is in his backpack. He shows it to me. Sure enough the wise and wonderful Gayle has made a little grid, with little icons depicting things like rest time and stories and outdoor play and lunch. And in each little space on the grid, Max has scribbled something. He cannot write but he is indeed working in his journal.

"Do you know what we need to do in about half an hour, after you and I are finished here, talking and reading?"

"No," says Max. "What?"

"We'll work on your birthday invitations, and you need to help write the names on the envelopes. And remember how many kids we said you could invite?"

"Fifty," says Max.

ON RETREAT

ALL IN GREEN WENT MY LOVE RIDING.
I wake with this line of poetry in my head, rolling through my memory, unprompted, over and over again. It is early and I am alone. Hector is away for a few days, now that term is over, with one of his choirs, doing seasonal concerts in small towns around the city.

I get up, put on my heavy robe and slippers and quietly go downstairs to make coffee. Jam is sleeping. Little Max is sleeping. The cats accompany me. The house is cold, and I turn up the heat. While I wait for the coffee I sit in the window seat and look at the snow. There is a lot of it already. I see no green. *All in green went my love riding.* Am I dreaming in green because it is winter and my sensibilities are rebelling? I try to remember the rest of the poem, a Cummings poem I have known for years, and I can get no further than the first line. This bothers me a little; I have taught this poem and should know it better. But I am sleepy, and often my memory is faulty first thing in the morning and last at night.

I work on it for a while, in a desultory manner. I can't get anywhere. It sounds so lovely in my mind. *All in green went my love riding.* Surely Hector could do something with this, set it to music. Once he is done *Patient Griselda,* of course, and the conclusion of that is nowhere in sight.

I get up quietly and head for the office to look up

the rest of the poem. I am perturbed that I did not remember the savage ending.

All in green went my love riding
on a great horse of gold
into the silver dawn.

four lean hounds crouched low and smiling
my heart fell dead before.

I am sitting, looking at the page, when Little Max appears and climbs up on me.

"Can I print something off the computer?"

"Good morning, Max."

"Can I?"

"Good morning, honey."

"Good morning, Mom. Can I?

I refuse to answer yet. "I love you, Max. How was your sleep?"

"Good. I love you, Mom. How was your sleep?"

"I slept well, honey. Thanks for asking. Yes, you can print off one page after breakfast." He groans. He pretends to hate breakfast.

His little fingernails scrabble at my shoulder and I catch his hand, gently, and look at him as firmly as I can without looking mean. He is an expert in the nuance of my looks. Once, when he was only two, I was upset about something, but thought I was hiding it perfectly well. All he had to do was glance at me, and then he said, "Why is your face so angry?"

Max and I eat breakfast and pull on our coats over our night things. This aberration delights him. It is holiday time, so I don't see why we cannot play in the snow in pyjamas. The snow is the wrong kind for moulding or shaping but Max enjoys kicking it, and I watch the sun move through the shower of flakes he creates around him, surging up around his little black boots. I shovel off the steps and the front walk, hoping my long wool coat is long enough to cover the fact that I have nothing but a nightgown underneath.

Jam comes out and offers to take Little Max on a sled ride to the bakery to get cinnamon buns. Everyone is delighted. I go back inside, take off my coat, climb the stairs and get back into bed. I am surprised by my own need to do this. It is a beautiful day. I can see the beauty. I really can. But I close my eyes on it.

I WONDER, BY MY TROTH, what thou and I did, till we loved.

This is today's line. It has been circulating in my head all night, or so it seems. At first it was a wondrous thing, but now I feel inhabited by it, in an almost sinister way. I wish Hector were here. I could give it to him – it is appropriate – and ask him to do something with it, and I could be freed from it.

At least I know that this poem is more benevolent. It has no pits for my affection to fall into and be chewed by wolves. But that is all I can remember. It really is a love poem. But I cannot remember the next line. I have taught this poem more than the other. I should know this one. I love John Donne.

It is still dark. Very dark. It is a terrible thing to feel like crying so soon after awakening. And stupid to be crying about a poem. I command myself to stop, and it works. I blow my nose. I realize that, strangely, I don't even want coffee this morning, and wonder why.

Yesterday I scraped the side of the car, backing it into the lane on the way to get groceries. Hector will not be happy. I have moved the car out of the garage a million times and never come close to damaging it before. There is no excuse for me. I close my eyes again, trying to shut out the ugly scratch. The scratch doesn't matter, but it does.

I examine my life and wonder what is the matter. All I can see is what ought to be health and happiness. Lovely boy, handsome and caring husband, blah blah blah. My mind wanders to Jam, sleeping in our living room. He is cheerful these days, a little subdued. He is busy. It is the Christmas season and there is plenty for musicians to do. He has seen Blanche rarely since he moved here. She knows he is waiting for her, that he came here for her. But something is raw, and she has told him she wants to think for a while. He is being remarkably patient, for Jam.

I am only forty-two. But my knees creak when I move around the house, especially in the mornings, and I have to flex my fingers to get them going. I think my kidneys are acting up. I'm getting old.

Little Max is calling me. He has wet the bed. He hates this, poor fellow. I heave myself out of bed in an unattractive manner, making a little grunt. If Hector were here, I would try not to do this. Not very sexy. Not sexy at all. But he is not here so I don't have to pretend I am a sylph. I am a flabby, middle-aged woman who grunts when she hauls herself out of bed. I am needed. That is something. My body moves on an automatic trajectory to my son's room. I am helpful.

"I THINK," SAYS JAKE, "that you might benefit from..." He stops to think.

From what? Shock treatments? Heavy-duty anti-depressants? I hope he doesn't suggest real therapy. I enjoy talking with Jake and I can't imagine starting over again with a counsellor. What I'm doing with Jake is not counselling. We drink coffee and talk. And I like to think that Jake finds it interesting too. After all I am a stimulating person with lots of interests. Aren't I?

"Have you ever thought about going on a retreat?" I shake my head. Apparently there are some friendly Benedictine nuns in town who are very welcoming to those who need to sit alone and do a little brooding. Or a lot of brooding. They don't judge. That's why they're nuns. I guess. "I think it would be good for you. You know, these memory things, and the way you are worried about your body and reaction times...it could just be stress. Sorry, Janey, I didn't mean to say 'just' stress. Not at all. And you should probably have a checkup soon. Maybe it's something else. But my hunch – and I could be wrong – is that it's stress."

Stress. What do I have to be tied up in knots about? I have no right to experience stress. A retreat sounds self-indulgent. Nevertheless, Jake makes the call and arranges for me to have a forty-eight-hour retreat a few days after Christmas. It is a quiet time, and Jam can help Hector entertain Little Max while the daycare is closed. No guilt. Apparently.

I go to meet Blanche for coffee, yet another cup I probably don't need, before she goes away to visit her parents for a week. She is quiet but apparently at ease. Serene. But who knows? Maybe I look serene to her, and I'm what? Numb? I feel a little frozen. We talk about Christmas.

"I can't remember much about Christmas from year to year. It always seems blurry to me. You know, there are people who can say, oh, that was the year we had the Fraser fir. That was the year the Sunday School had the hayride. But Christmas is just this mildly pleasant, slightly irritating blur to me." I realize I have never opened up this much to Blanche before, and change the subject. "Little Max is so excited. Last year he didn't quite get it. But now that he is four. Oh boy. He's had Santa's Nanaimo bars out and ready for him since Monday. I had to convince him not to leave out a glass of milk already. Instead, Santa is getting a Coke. Which he probably doesn't want. Often Santa wants a martini."

While I talk, the line of the latest poem to befuddle me is circulating in my mind. *How oft, when thou, my music, music play'st.* Blanche is looking at her coffee cup. I'm not sure she is listening to me talk about Christmas, and that's okay. I'm not saying anything anyway. I watch her use the tip of her little finger to try to capture some of the foam from the edge of her cappuccino. I am babbling. Maybe she has something that she'd like to say. So we sit in a reasonably companionable silence. I know the line is Shakespeare, and it is an obscure sonnet, so I am not that worried about this memory lapse. But Hector, as a grad student, set it to music, and I used to hear it all the time, so I should know it. But I can't get past the first line.

When Blanche does speak, I am surprised at what she says. "Beatrice Haight made a pass at me."

"What?"

"Well, I think it might have been a pass. She asked

me to her house for Christmas Eve, and the tone was...unexpected. It wasn't like she was asking a friend or a colleague, but like she was asking me on a date. You know? It's hard to explain. But I think I got the intention right. Has she ever been married? I really didn't think of her as being...Sapphic." She laughs and then we both do, and have a hard time stopping.

"Yeah, she was married once. I think. I don't know much about it. And I'm with you. I wouldn't have guessed. Hey, that's sort of cool. I like her more," I say. "But what did you say?"

"Oh, I could say, in all honesty, that I just couldn't, since I'm going away. But if it was really what I think it was, that won't end it, will it?" Blanche smiles at me. "You've been very sweet, Janey, and Hector too. Not to ask me about Jam. I know he's there, in your midst, and the subject must be, well, sort of an obvious one to want to ask about. But you haven't pressed me about him. And I'm grateful."

She looks out the window of the Neighbourhood Café. It is a brilliant December day. The sun is blinding. Indeed, I am still wearing my sunglasses since we are by the window and I was tired of shading my eyes. "I think in January I'll be ready to talk with him some more. I feel like I've been such a – such a Little Miss, you know? But I needed some solitude, and I feel pretty good these days. And I know he is there, and I care about how he feels. So, if he asks, tell him that I'll come see him when I get back from holidays. Okay?"

I nod. She has not fished for information about Jam. She is too dignified for that. But I feel, out of loyalty to him, as if I should say something about his state of mind. I consider carefully.

"Jam," I begin, "used to be a pain in the ass. Charming, but a pain. Very charming. But he's different now. I don't know how to explain it. But I like him more now." I decide that is enough. "Anyway."

We smile at each other.

"When you came here," I say, "I wanted to hate you. Raven-haired beauty. Everything I wanted to be, and cannot be. So poised. But I've never been able to hate you. I'm always looking for rivals, I guess. Hector is – Hector is absurdly handsome, don't you think? I always think that there is someone around the corner who will take him away from me."

She looks a little mystified. "Hector is good-looking, I guess. But so are you, Janey. I don't know why you would think like that."

Good-looking! It is my turn to be mystified. Hector is more than just good-looking. He is a gorgeous romantic catastrophe waiting to happen. His bones don't creak when he gets out of bed in the mornings. And lately, he is a dynamo of priapism and I cannot keep up.

But I do not, of course, tell Blanche this.

THE PLACE IS FULL OF WOMEN. I hadn't thought about this. It is not anything like an official women's retreat, but there are no men wanting to brood during this Christmas season. I head into my room and shut the door. I have already laid out or put away my things. Didn't take long. Notebook. Novel. Helpful spiritual tome. Slippers. Sensible cotton lounging clothes. I like my cell, but it really is a cell. White and spare. No pictures. Just a cross. I like it, but I'm glad I won't be here long.

I lie on the bed and imagine I am a nun. I wonder how many nuns have slept in this room and what their thoughts were. I try to imagine I am a young nun. None of the nuns I've seen so far here are young in the least. All middle-aged and older. All short too. Why is that? They are reserved with the guests, but I have heard them in the kitchen, laughing. The place is very quiet and meditative, but occasionally I hear bursts of jollity from the nuns' quarters. I like them.

A young nun. With what sort of desires? It seems so adolescent of me to leap immediately to the question of sex. If I really had any understanding of nuns, I would know that probably the sexual question is far from being the primary one. But maybe I am a perpetual adolescent. Could I be a nun? Sometimes I am less keen, lately, on sex than Hector is. Will my desire eventually drain away and then would I be a good candidate for this place? Or has their desire not gone away in the least? Is it still there every day, part of their being, and they have to deal with it, like the rest of us?

I reach out to wrap Hector and Little Max in blessing. I do this when I am away from them. It doesn't seem enough merely to pray for them. I try to picture them, their entire bodies, and then I wrap them in my love, like a long piece of cloth. Somehow. Anyway, it works for me. I apologize to them. I am so sorry, I say. I am so sorry.

IT SEEMS TO ME THAT *we have something here.*

I wake up four hours later. It is the middle of the day, and I've had an enormous nap. This is a little perturbing. Not to mention the voice I've heard. I can still hear it echoing. *It seems to me that we have something here.*

I peer around. No one, of course. The hallway outside the closed door of my cell seems quiet. Was it my own voice? Maybe. Was I talking in my sleep? This seems possible. I listen to the timbre of the voice in my memory. It seems ungendered.

Oh God, I really am cracking up. I'm hearing voices. Then I hear the appellation I've used, and stop. Start over again. I say it out loud, sitting on the edge of the bed in my nun's cell. "Oh God. Am I cracking up? Help."

There, I've turned it over to God. God's problem now. I stretch, and feel a great need for coffee. I run my fingers through my hair, pull the door open and peer into the hallway.

I patter down towards the lounge where, I was told, there would always be coffee and fruit and cookies. I open the door, and there are millions of women. I hesitate. No, there are only six. But it seems like more. The visitors are, I was told, mostly on silent retreat, but these women are not silent. There are four of them muttering away to each other, while the other two appear to be reading. But they keep looking up. Waiting for their turn to leap in. They want to talk too.

I don't. I get some coffee, stir it, stare out the window at the bird feeder. Two of the women are talking about food intolerances. They compare grains I've never heard of, talk about where to get various exotic substances. "I toss them in salads, in bread, in muffins." I do remember the last time I made a salad, but I cannot remember the last time I made muffins, and I've never made bread. "And then I went a whole week without milk of any sort, meat, eggs or wheat.

And you would not believe how much better I felt." I get the feeling everyone is talking around the issue of diarrhea, but there is a women's code or something that forbids the use of the word.

One of them appears at my side, and I look down at her. I am at least a foot taller. She has short dark hair and a very earnest expression. An expression of sorrow. I can see that instantly, even though she is smiling. "I'm Albertine."

"Janey. Nice to meet you."

"Are you Silent?"

I hesitate. I had not actually decided. Jake had not recommended silence. Just the retreat part. "Not really."

Before five minutes are over, I am booked to go for a wintry walk with Albertine right after supper. This is not what I had intended at all. I murmur something and duck out, wandering into the chapel on the way back to my room. It is dark in here, with one candle in a red glass holder in a wall sconce and some small stained glass windows providing the only light. It is an interesting room, and I sit down in the middle of the space and let my mind wander. *It seems to me that we have something here.*

I don't look around this time. I have come to the conclusion that I am hearing my own voice somehow. I try not to worry about the origin and think about the sentence. *It seems to me.* Not very heartening. Not positive. Not positive at all. But then: *we.* I'm in this with somebody. That's good. *Something.* A vague word. Still, better than *nothing.*

My mind heads down a byway. I work over the lyrics to the song "Something Good" from *The Sound of Music* in my mind. I can do that fine. I can remember any Rodgers and Hammerstein lyric. Just not anything important. But then I see Maria and the Captain, facing each other and singing, and I feel chagrin at my disloyalty to a grand movie moment.

I come to the last word of my hallucinatory sentence. *Here.* In this retreat centre? In this body? In this heart? I am thinking all this over when suddenly I realize I have been half asleep, sitting on a chair in the middle of this chapel. I never fall asleep sitting up.

I stand, return to my room and consider falling into bed and going back to sleep. Maybe later. I hold it in reserve, as a treat. Instead, I sit at the desk and open the envelope that Hector has given me. "Open it later," he said. "I was going to give it to you for Christmas. But when you decided to go on retreat, I thought this would be a good gift for that. Open it when you've been there awhile. And think of me. I'll be thinking of you."

I open it. It is a little piece of music, in his own hand. He has written a melody to the Donne poem I told him I was struggling with. *I wonder, by my troth, what thou and I did until we loved. For Janey.* I try to pick out the melody on my own. I can tell he has written it in my range, fairly low. I go back to the chapel with the manuscript paper in my hand, and on the piano pick out the melody very softly, with one hand, standing, humming.

AT SUPPER THE WOMEN ARE VERY CHIRPY. I think they arrived around the same time as I did, but they appear to know everything about each other already. They mutter about men. No one but me seems to have a husband any more. I dare not mention mine, nor how much I already miss him.

I try to think of something to say. I have abandoned any pretence of silence. There is a silent group, on their own in the corner, but I have sat with the talkers. Might as well. But I am unsure of retreat etiquette. Am I supposed to be spilling my guts to these strangers? They all seem to be.

One of them is listing all the faiths she has embraced in her life. Not purposefully, but as a side issue to another conversation. "I grew up Baptist. My sister and I became Anglicans. Then I was a Lutheran for a while. And Calvary Temple. Now I go to a Catholic church, but I'm really a Jain."

I try to smile at this. She is beaming at me and telling the table about her three disastrous marriages, which are really her main subject. Am I supposed to smile at such statements of faith? Of lack of faith? If I smile, I'm encouraging her in her religious waywardness. She is pleased with herself. She thinks she has broadened her horizons. Well, maybe she has. Who am I to judge? The woman on the other side is recommending spiritual classics for us all to read. Merton. John of the Cross. I try to block her out. I read all the time. I'm here not to read, I decide. I'm here to listen to the nice voices in my head. Now she is recommending Robert Graves, and I cannot help myself. I snort.

"Worst book I ever read." I dilute my nastiness with a winning smile, and put another heaping spoonful of mashed potatoes on my plate. The Graves woman is nonplussed, and I decide to change the subject. "Does anyone know what that little brown and light yellow bird is, that comes to the bird feeder?"

They all have opinions. An opinion about a bird in the vicinity of a retreat centre is something everyone must have. Standard equipment. If this were not a winter retreat, they would also be able to compare notes on prairie wildflowers. There is a buzz of conversation, and I am safe to head back into my own thoughts, and into my meal, which I am enjoying tremendously. I did not know nuns were such good cooks. A kind of sweet and sour chicken. Superb. There is a new voice at my side, and I turn to look at the young woman beside me. She is the only one here who is more or less close to my age, and she has been, hitherto, even more reserved than me.

"How long have you been on retreat?"

"Just today," I say. I notice that I do not offer the information that I am a university professor, nor that I have lost my memory. Others offer their reasons for being here. "And I've never done it before. What about you?"

"Oh, lots of times." I have already heard this from the other women. Everyone except me, it seems, goes on retreat as regularly as getting a haircut. Or getting laid, I think privately. "And this is Day Five. Day Five is always when things start to open up for me."

I look at her. She can't be more than thirty, although there is something in her demeanour that looks both younger and older. Her name is Honey. The lines around her eyes tell conflicting stories. They are the lines of someone who once smiled a lot, but I see no trace of recent smile activity. I ask her about Day Five as we move to the lounge with cups of tea.

"On Day Five," she says, "I stop fighting it. Fighting with my sense that I should be somewhere else.

Fighting with God. I stop wondering what is going on elsewhere. I stop counting the days until the end. I can just sort of..."

"Be?" I supply what seems to me the natural conclusion to the sentence, but she smiles, very slightly, and shakes her head.

"No. I was actually going to say *die*. Just a little though. I think sometimes we need to die a little, shed our bad selves like a snake's skin. We need to let the old, harmful lives die. And then I wait, to see what new life might come for me."

It sounds awfully passive, I want to say. And morbid, Honey. She looks rather cheerful as she tells me about her retreat regimen. Lots of rituals of inner cleansing and waiting for release from spiritual toxins. I like her. I really do. She has an honest face. I look around at the other women. Several of them are planning some kind of healing circle for later this evening. They explain the rite. There will be a talking stone handed from person to person, and you wait to see what will be released when it is handed to you. I have to get out of here. But I look at their faces and they are all good faces. Honest faces, like Honey's. But faces, for the most part, that have known too much suffering. They are enjoying being in the company of each other's suffering a little too much.

I feel pretty healthy and excuse myself.

ALBERTINE IS A RETIRED SCHOOLTEACHER. She is only fifty-five. No kids. She is polite enough to ask me a few questions about myself, and I give brief responses, enough information to be cordial, not unfriendly. I have a boy, recently turned four. Sometimes I have a tough time with him. My husband and I are both terribly busy with our careers, but we love our work, although it can be frustrating. My family is large but scattered. I picture the fragments of my family across the continent. Scattered like little pieces of paper. Like a torn-up cheque. I wonder why I picture them in this way. My father is dead, I say, and my mother has remarried and moved to New Zealand. I give Albertine these autobiographical offerings but they seem odd. Not quite right. They are not who I am. They are not why I'm here.

She talks about food issues some more. About meditation. I think back to the many food conversations I had with women when I was breast-feeding Max. Women would tell about the things they had eaten, and how the food entered the baby's system, and how they could tell all sorts of things from what the baby's poop looked like. Food. Food. Food. Do men talk about food so much, their own digestive systems? Consult their entrails? I think of the men I know. Mostly they just eat. It is only an hour since supper, and Albertine is making me hungry again. I wonder if there is more of that pineapple upside-down cake.

Albertine is saying something about a visit to the site of the Crystal Palace, in England. I nod, and then get a shivery feeling. "Crystal Palace" was one of the phrases I wrote, sort of automatically, when I started to talk with Jake this summer. I didn't know what it meant at the time and I still don't know. But it has just arrived.

I decide it is a gift, a gift I don't know what to do with. But a gift nevertheless; sometimes these things arrive and we are supposed to say thank you. It might come in useful or not. Not everything has to be useful to be valuable. I take deep breaths of winter air. It is a moderate evening, not too bad really. Apparently Albertine is going to go snowshoeing tomorrow. She invites me and I decline. Although I've always wanted to do it. But not tomorrow.

WHEN WE'VE BEEN THERE TEN THOUSAND YEARS, *bright shining as the sun.*
    It is still dark, although nearly seven, and the bells for the nuns' morning prayers will surely go soon. Or have they gone already? I listen to this new line, which has been in my head for a while. I don't know how long, in my half-sleeping, half-waking state. I am tired of sleeping. I had two naps yesterday. I get up.
    I know the rest of this verse, easily. *We've no less days to sing God's praise than when we first begun.* This is promising, even though it is a hymn I have sung my whole life, and so is part of my bones and therefore, I tell myself, not really a feat of remembrance. But I feel a kind of lightening. I sing the verse to myself, and then all of "Amazing Grace," or most of it. I can remember most of it. I scan, internally, the words to my own line, as I think of it, the one that was with me in sleep. *When we've been there ten thousand years, bright shining as the sun.* There is that *we* again. Do I want to probe it, define it? Not really. God and I? My neuroses and I? Hector and I? I know it is not this at all. Although it is, and it isn't. I stop probing. Leave it alone, Janey. *We* is good. I look at *there* for a while, comparing it to the

here I heard yesterday. *It seems to me that we have something here.* How do we get from here to there? God, I ask silently, how do I get from *here* to *there*?

I think I know, and stop thinking. I caress the line *bright shining as the sun* for a while. I remember loving it as a child. The way the melody soared up to *sun*. I stop thinking. At this same moment, I believe, all the words to the first few lines of the sonnet, my lost sonnet, arrive. Just like that.

> *How oft, when thou, my music, music play'st*
> *Upon that blessed wood whose motion sounds*
> *With thy sweet fingers, when thou gently sway'st*
> *The concord that mine ear confounds*

That's as far as I can get. But it's pretty good. I feel pretty good.

JANUARY

COMMITTEE WORK

"I HEAR YOU WERE ON RETREAT IN DECEMBER, JANET. Did you enjoy it?" Beatrice Haight settles herself at the head of the table in the committee room. I try to imagine her lusting after Blanche. Or anyone for that matter. It is a stretch. It is more than a stretch. It is an incredible elongation. Nope. Can't do it.

"Very much, thank you. It was lovely." Listen to me. Gracious Janey. Pass the petits fours, Janey. But I do feel gracious. I can afford to extend every courtesy to poor old Beatrice. I have spent the last ten days or so being endlessly encased in the connubial embrace. I feel worn out with love, pleasantly so. If I thought Hector was stirred up before I went on retreat, that was nothing to how he was on my return. You'd think I'd been gone for a month or a year. He claimed it was the thought that I was pretending to be a nun that drove him particularly crazy. When I got home, he was always encouraging me to drape dark towels over my head, and then he'd leap on me. He hasn't been this randy since after Max was born. The unaccustomed extent of my breasts, then, had an astonishing effect on him. "Wow," he kept saying. "Wow." It was a delirious time, what with all the sex and all the sleeplessness. We had to invent new ways to have sex, of course, because I was supposed to be in my confinement or something, but there are a million different ways to have sex.

Beatrice is speaking to me again. Oh dear. What did

she say? I thought she was speaking to Lonely Lyle, our forlorn linguistics guy. His classes are always so under-subscribed, and every term he gets more droopy. "Pardon me, Beatrice? I'm sorry."

I am being asked for my ideas, "original ones," says Beatrice pointedly, for fundraising. The Department's scholarship fund is, reportedly, standing at about forty-seven dollars and ninety-five cents. This committee is, strictly speaking, supposed to be handing out awards and deciding on the terms of said awards, but unless someone does some fundraising, the students will go hungry. They will not be able to top up their phone cards. Their ring-tone expenditures will cease. The manufacturers who supply all their little beaded hemp bracelets will starve.

Concentrate, Janey. On the task at hand. Fundraising. Not my strong suit. It is hard to think, with the waves of frostiness emanating from Beatrice. I propose the name of an illustrious alumna of the Department and get the others thinking about who knows her best. Could we get her to come and be part of an event? I stay out of the discussion and think about putting on *Patient Griselda* as a fundraiser. It might be fun, but probably not ready soon enough. Mentally, I tick through the usual list: talent show, bake sale, raffle. All stupid. We'd raise a couple of hundred.

I swivel my chair back and forth to get their attention. "Why don't we send letters to all the current faculty and all the retirees, and a few carefully hand-picked friends of the Department, and ask them each to give a hundred dollars? The only work will be the mailing list, and Kate can help with that. Let's write a very simple and brief letter that basically says: the responsible thing to do is give us one hundred dollars now, and thank you very much. Let's see, ask one hundred people for one hundred dollars...that's –" I turn an appealing eye to Lyle. Linguist. Must be good with numbers too.

"Ten thousand," says Lyle.

"Wow. Really? Ten thousand. Sounds like a lot. But even if half the people give one hundred (and who is going to give less? We can all easily afford that), we've got five thousand, and we can squeak through for this year. Right?"

There is silence. Stupid too, evidently. But no. Beatrice is tapping her coffee cup in a forthright manner. I know this tic well. She is pleased.

Maybe I will no longer be the baby in this Department. Maybe they'll let me chair the awards committee someday, when Beatrice retires or goes to that big colloquium in the sky.

I DECIDE TO TELL JAKE ABOUT my erotic dreams about students. I am unprepared for his response.

A chortle, and then another chortle. And a sort of yelp. "Is that all, Janey? Naughty dreams about teenage boys? Is that all we've got to talk about, Janey? I declare you to be a happy and normal human being." He laughs again, leans towards me, playfully punches me on the shoulder. "Hey, get out there, Janey. Tear into that world. Chew it up. Yum. You are now as healthy as any asshole you can name."

I love this about Jake. He is both one of the holiest

people I have ever met and one of the most profane. He is so clearly relieved by my state of mind that he is getting a little giddy, and I know, for the first time, how worried he was about me. I am relieved too, seeing myself, a little, from his point of view. I now realize that he had stopped swearing in front of me for the last few months. His foul mouth means that I am okay. He hugs me, deliberately bouncing his largish stomach against mine, laughing.

I AM WORKING ON A PAPER about talking animals in Canadian children's books. I am hoping to give it at a children's literature conference that will be held here, later in the spring. I have retained the services of René as my unpaid research assistant. Whenever he comes over to babysit, I sit down with him and pump him about books he read as a kid. He read everything, and he has perfect recall. He treats the books and their talking animals with great seriousness, never making fun of anything, treating all characters as having equal worth. Hearing him discuss Mrs. Tabitha Twitchit in Beatrix Potter's *Tom Kitten* is precious. He's very good at reading Potter to Little Max. Potter is difficult to get right, with its sudden outbursts of violence and odd slant on reality. My favourite line in the book is when Tabitha Twitchit says to her kittens that she is "affronted" by their behaviour. René's favourite page is when the kittens have to come by degrees up the rockery and their clothes come off. What is a rockery? We both wonder.

"But there aren't very many talking animals in Canadian books," he says. "Not like in British ones – *The*

Wind in the Willows, Narnia, *Black Beauty.*"

"Does Beauty talk? I didn't remember that."

"I don't see why you would concentrate on the Canadian books, if they are so realistic. It's a kind of non-issue, isn't it?"

"Ah, René, that's where you have to learn about academic conferences. It is far more fun to present a research project about something that is not there than something that is. I can get people all riled up, outraged. Where are the talking animals? Who has repressed the talking animals? I could make my scholarly reputation."

René listens to me with solemn attention. He takes everything so seriously I am a little sorry to be acting the professorial fool. But I am only half kidding.

I DREAM I ACQUIRE A LITERARY AGENT for my mystery novel, which is only about fifteen pages long so far. But I have a title: *Death by Non-Confidence Motion.* That part is for real. But in my dream, I am in a Manhattan high-rise, talking to my literary agent, wearing a darling wide-brimmed black straw hat with a contrasting wide white ribbon. It perfectly matches my black silk cocktail dress, because I am about to step out to the Algonquin to meet a few friends. It is a dress that actually has a crinoline, a white one, and in my dream it is not scratchy, as I've always imagined crinolines to be, but soft. It makes a whispering noise when I cross my legs that is quite delightful. The neckline of this dress is low and elegant. The era of the dress is about 1947. Is it 1947? Probably.

Nothing really happens, and I wake up. What strikes

me about this dream is that I could feel the silk of the dress and the swoosh of the crinoline. It was a very palpable dream. I could even smell things. I wonder where the details came from. I think I had a Barbie doll with a similar outfit when I was about seven, but this dream crinoline is surely exaggerated.

Hector appears in the doorway with two cups of coffee, pushing open the door with his toe, very carefully. He is wearing a shawl of mine wrapped around his hips, and it is too long. "Nearly killed me coming up the stairs," he says. The wrap is very attractive on him, the way women's things often look nicer on men, but I tug at the wrap anyway and he climbs back into bed without it. I tell him about my dream. He claims not to know what a crinoline is.

"Today," says Hector, "I am going to finish *Patient Griselda.*"

"Really? Are you that close?"

"Not particularly. But I'm going to finish it if it kills me. It's been lurking too long. I know the scoring and detail work will take a lot longer, but I want to finish up on the basic melodic work. And put it aside for a while." He scrunches up his mouth. I can barely see him in the lamplight. Although our curtains are open, it is still dark this early in the morning. "Griselda is bothering me. She is the kind of accommodating monster that enables the tyrants of the world. Hitler needed lots of Griseldas, of both sexes, around him. She is a masochist of the top order, and I knew that when I started, but I didn't think it would bother me so much." He hesitates. "And Janey, I really did want you to sing it, but I think it would be bad for you to attempt it. She's so – so – anyway, the fun has gone out of it."

I think about this ancient story from Chaucer: the woman whose devotion is tested by an unworthy husband. Hector does not want to refer too often to my recent bouts with anxiety or stress, or whatever they were. Or are. I kiss him. "I am quite capable of separating myself from Griselda. She's an interesting idea to me, an idea to explore. She's not real to me, Hector. And I would never emulate her, or allow her to swallow me up. Whether I can sing the part is another thing. I can, around here, for you, anyway. And we'll sort out the rest later."

"I have to admit," he says, "that I do like the part where the husband makes her take off all her clothes. That is a good part. That's the only good part. Let's rehearse that, Janey. I'm your director, now. You have to listen."

"Parsnip," I say, "do I have any clothes on?"

He pretends to have just noticed that I do not. "Hey. Good Griselda! You go to the top of the biddable wife competition! Now it's your turn. What do you want of your impatient husband?"

Little Max enters, right on cue. Hector groans. I cover up the two of us with a sheet, rather inadequately. I sing "Good Morning" from *Singin' in the Rain,* loudly, to conceal Hector's groans, which are a little rude.

"Is it time to go?" asks Max. I think, looking at him, that I will stop calling him Little Max soon. The child has grown enormously in the past month or so. And his vocabulary is something else. He used the word "penance" the other day, and correctly, more or less. I suppose he heard it in church, but if so, he must be the only child listening. The rest of them are always

rustling their tissue-paper flowers and crashing their
Hot Wheels together.

I look at the clock. "Not yet, but I suppose we
should get a move on. I'll lay out your clothes for you,
honey. And then go and immerse my long and hungry
body in a deep, hot tub." More groaning from Hector,
who rolls over on his stomach. "Do you want to get
going early today for some reason?"

Max does a little dance on the spot. "Yes! We're
walking to the Millennium Library. I have to be there
by nine fifteen. At the latest. That's what Gayle said."

"Walking? Or going in strollers and wagons and
stuff?"

"Oh, Mom. Strollers don't go in the snow. No.
We're walking."

"Really?" I turn to Hector. "Do you know about this?"

He groans some more. "All I know about," he mutters into his pillow, "is a subject that I cannot at the
current time enlarge upon."

"Wow," I say, and reach over to stroke his but-
tocks, through the sheet. I think I do it casually, but
Max spots me and comes over and does it too. I wig-
gle around and create a kind of sheath dress from the
abandoned shawl, stand up. "It's incredible that kids
can walk so far. I guess you guys are more grown up
than I thought." I glance at Hector. "We'd better
leave Daddy alone," I say cheerfully. "Let's go eat
Fruit Loops."

"WHAT IF I SAID THAT THE BEST WAY to recognize a
postmodern novel is to ask it if it is very aware of

itself?" I flap my own copy of Rushdie's *Midnight's Children* at my Twentieth-Century Novel class. "How would that work as a definition?"

Discussion staggers on for a while, and then stops. At this rate we'll never get anywhere. Which is probably appropriate for the topic. The postmodern novel course that went in circles and ate itself. I look down at my notes, the usual melee of scribbled questions that I hope to launch into the classroom atmosphere and that will then explode into endless fireworks of fascinating and insightful discussions. Once in a while, it happens. Almost.

These teaching notes aren't going to work today, however. I look out at their desks and note that a good number of the students don't even have the Rushdie novel here. Great. I decree it is group-work time. I divide them into four groups of six or seven and ask that they find one passage that demonstrates that this is a postmodern novel and one passage that argues that this is not. There should be at least a couple of students in each group who have actually read the thing, and maybe they'll be able to act as trail guides for the others.

I have ten minutes to myself and perch on the edge of my desk while discussion gurgles in the room, dries up, is stoppered and gurgles some more. I speed-read the draft of the English Department's five-year plan. There's a big Department meeting tomorrow. The plan has been drafted by Lonely Lyle, our forlorn linguistics guy, and feels like it too. I also feel like I've been reading documents like this my entire life, and they all smudge together. I realize I haven't registered any of it, and turn back to the beginning again. There is someone at my elbow, and I turn to look at him.

It is Luke, the kid I've had dreams about. Well, not lately, now that I think about it. But anyway, there he is, scowling a little. "Janey," he says, "there are only five minutes left and our group is going nowhere. And I've got a nihilism paper due in my evening class tonight and I'd really rather be proofreading it." Luke never calls me Dr. Janey, as about half the students do.

"Sure," I say. "Nihilism. Sweet. Off you go. Have fun." He takes off and I remind myself not to look at his bum. "Okay, everyone. Remember to bring back the results of what your group figured out. We'll look at this at the top of next class. And don't forget to bring me some chocolate next time, because I think I might be having my period and I'll be really cantankerous." I don't think anyone hears this last part, because nearly all of them are out of the door already, and the rest are hooting about something. I pack up my stuff and head back to my office.

Tom is waiting outside my door. I know that his schedule of History courses often meshes with mine this term, and we're both done for the day. "Have time for a beer?" he asks. I dump my books and we head down the hall to the faculty club. "Actually," he says, "I have a little work to talk about first. I think we have a student in common, and I want to ask you about him." Tom looks around us and drops his voice. "Luke Frederickson. Know him?"

"Yeah." It's my Luke, as I often privately think of him. Or used to. "He's a sharp kid. Very sharp. Which of your classes is he in?"

"Western Civ." We're in the faculty club now, and although it is only four, the place is packed. We wedge ourselves into a back corner, near the popcorn machine, and scoop ourselves a few bowls. The entire Theology Department, all male of course, is perched on stools near the bar, so it can gaze with admiration at the beautiful bartender, Julia. Tom gets us our beers, having to elbow nearly all the university's philosophers to get up to the counter. It is only Tuesday. It's late January. Don't these people have anything to do?

"I've never had him before, but I know he has a reputation for cleverness. So imagine my surprise when he hands in his first assignment – a pretty straightforward thing on early economic systems – and it's plagiarized."

"No way. Not him. The guy doesn't need to plagiarize. Really, he's one of the best students I've ever had. He knows how to do original research. And he's a really fine writer. Are you sure, Tom?"

"It was all too obvious. Another student had just quoted from the same reference work, so it was all fresh in my mind. But Luke had plunked in huge chunks of this reference work, unattributed. Just plunked them in. Rather clumsily, I thought."

"That doesn't sound right." I take a swig of my beer, and think back to my recent encounters with Luke. He has been a little odd, maybe, but he's always been chippy towards me. So I don't know what his regular demeanour really is, or if his attitude towards me is his usual attitude. "You know what, Tom? It sounds like a smart kid trying to get caught."

"Yeah?"

"I've only seen it once before. It had to go to the discipline committee, which was unfortunate because it was a very particular case. But this could be the same. I suppose it still has to come up before the committee."

"Why would he do it?"

"Sometimes they appear so grown up, you know," I say, "but it's like their sensibilities get stretched to breaking point because they're not nearly as sophisticated as they think they have to be. This Luke guy has quite a chunk of armour on him. I think it's getting heavy. I think he wants attention, some help getting it off."

Tom is grateful for my help, and I duck across the street in the whirling snow to pick up Max. I try not to breathe my beer breath on the daycare workers. Damn, I'm glad I have a job where I can legitimately drink beer with my colleagues at the end of the day and not, instead, supervise the tidying away of play clay or wipe yet another pudding-covered face. I worship these daycare workers. They should be paid seventy million dollars a day. Max shows me his art project, two sheets of construction paper crunched together into a protuberance and fastened with about six rolls of masking tape. He calls it "World." I praise it, and he says thank you. My heart nearly stops beating. *He says thank you.*

"You know," I say, as the credits roll on one of our favourite old *Star Trek* episodes. "That Shatner was one good-looking guy."

"Of course he was. Is," says Hector. "He's my father."

"You never told me."

"When my father was at his most agonizingly tedious, when I was growing up, I liked to fantasize that Captain Kirk was my father. It got me through some bad times."

"You never told me that," I repeat, and stretch my legs out on the couch, touching Hector's thigh lightly with my toes. "Jam, did he ever tell you that?"

Jam is lying on the floor at our feet. He has been trying to get one of the cats to function as a pillow while we watched Kirk and Spock. He yawns, sits up and roots in his belly button to clean out the lint. I close my eyes. I wish he would stop.

"No," Jam says, "but Hector did tell me that Jane Russell was his mother. Do you remember, Hec, those Cross-Your-Heart bra commercials she used to do? Those bras looked like two granaries tied together with elastic. In retrospect, they had no appeal at all. But at the time, hoo doggie, that was *it*. Jane Russell."

"Howard Hughes designed special aerodynamic brassieres for her, back in the thirties or forties or something," I offer.

"Janey knows all this stuff. Why do you know that, Janey?" Hector looks at me admiringly. "Let's make money off her. Let's put her on *Jeopardy* or something. What can you win a lot of money at, like Charlie Van Doren did on *Twenty-One,* way back when?"

"*Jeopardy* would do," says Jam.

"Thank you for thinking of exploiting me," I say. "It's really very sweet. But I couldn't. I'm all tied up with my singing career."

Jam belches, and I roll my eyes at Hector. Jam has been teaching Max to burp loudly, but I can't bring myself to complain about this, since Jam is spending lots of time with Max, teaching him some chords on his guitar, and a little bit of clarinet. The clarinet lessons sound like cats dying in the coils of venomous snakes, and the sounds make our own cats tear around the house in a very agitated manner. But still, Max is enjoying himself.

"Speaking of mothers," I say. "I have decided not to kill off a replica of my mother-in-law in a murder mystery."

"Really!" Hector sits up. "I thought you were enjoying writing that, Janey."

"For a while. But it's served its purpose. I don't think I'm cut out for murder and mayhem. And really, I shouldn't be bashing away at poor Mavis. She's not so bad. She's taught me a lot about colour coordination. And she gave me you." Jam snorts and heads for the door, pointing at my ill-assorted lounging things (leopard-print pants, striped green and white socks, blue hoodie) and saying good night.

When he is gone, I say it again. "She gave me you." I move in close to Hector, touching his collarbone. "I think I was jealous for a while, because I would think – Hector used to live inside her! That's what I want! I want Hector! And then of course, it came to me. I can have you anytime I want. Can't I, carrot?"

There is a noise in the hallway. Hector clears his throat and calls out. "I know it's you, Jam. Bugger off and go to bed so I can have knowledge of my wife."

Jam sings a little bit of "Too Darn Hot" and thumps down the stairs. "Good night, boys and girls," he shouts.

"He'll wake up the baby," I say through my teeth.

"No, he won't. It's eleven thirty. Max has been sleeping for hours. He never wakes up at this point. Hey, do you realize that Jam must have been celibate now for at least – oh, I don't know – two months? That's a monkish existence for him."

"Are you sure?"

"He's been here steadily. He's never disappeared for a night. He's had no opportunity that I can see. And no motive. He doesn't want anyone else. He wants her. He's waiting."

"It's adorable," I say. "Now shut up about Jam."

I DREAM THAT I AM A DICKENS CHARACTER. I am, I think, David Copperfield, although I'm not sure how I know this. And I am in love with a dragonfly, a lovely blue dragonfly. It is not a big dragonfly. Just a normal size. Occasionally it looks like Tinkerbell, but for most of the dream it looks like a dragonfly. I wake up.

I write it in my dream book, a journal I recently started, although I cannot see what possible meaning this one could have. But I'm not using the dream book for analysis so much as for storage. I have dropped the idea of the murder mystery, but I have a new popular-genre book I want to try. Fantasy. My title is *Emoticon*. That's all I've got so far, but I figure I'd better start storing up dreams. I know very little about the fantasy genre, but I've decided that this ignorance is in my favour. It will make me fresh.

My most promising dream so far involves boxes. An endlessly huge room, full of cardboard boxes, in towers that keep falling on me. I also have one where I am worshipped as a goddess on a very rocky island, where children bring me coffee cups as acts of homage. I'm not sure what use these dreams will be, but I note them all down.

Max and Hector take off in the car, and I walk to the Neighbourhood Café, where I am supposed to have a meeting with Luke. He lives nearby. I have claimed that he and I need to consult about the Department's literary dunk tank at the Arts Spring Fair, which he and I are jointly running. The dunk tank, not the fair. The fair involves a stage with big-name musical acts, tattoo booths, drinking and vomiting, the works. The English Department's contribution is fairly minor. And Luke and I haven't done anything yet. A good reason for a meeting. I think I will gently talk around the plagiarism thing, without mentioning it directly, and see what I can find out.

Luke is there, looking very young in the winter morning light. He is drinking tea and looks pale. I look at the book he is reading. *Wild Animals I Have Known.* He looks embarrassed, and quite rightly, I think. I look quizzical. "It's for Can Lit. We're supposed to do a report on popular children's stuff."

I drink the biggest latté on the menu and feel my heart start moving. Luke still looks pale. His tea has no firepower. We come up with a list of local celebrities to ask to participate in the literary dunk tank. They will be suspended over a tank of water and if they can't answer really simple questions of fact about literary works, they get dunked. For example, we ask Evelyn Hart of the ballet what Hamlet's mother's name was. Gertrude. She doesn't get dunked. We ask her how much Walt Whitman's brain weighed after death. She doesn't know. She gets dunked. That sort of thing. It will be in April, an AIDS hospice fundraiser. It will still be chilly, which is supposed to be part of the fun. I realize he is not looking at me much, but looking at the artwork over my left ear, and also down at the table.

"You seem unusual today, Luke. Is anything bothering you?" I know from several years of working with students now that you shouldn't ask if they are okay. You will get the automatic affirmative, and you have to keep digging. If you start with the negative "Are you worried about something?" often you get to the nub of the matter faster. Possibly this is bad counselling etiquette, but I'm an amateur. It works for me.

Luke immediately looks relieved. "How did you know something was wrong?" I shrug. Never say too much in a situation like this. Listen. Be careful and kind and listen. "I really have been wanting to say something to you for a long time, Janey. But I thought I shouldn't, and I don't know how anyway. But it is – it is – a vexation." He grins, weakly. Vexation is a word I used a lot last term in the Nineteenth-Century Novel, especially when talking about Dickens. It is one of my pet words. He hesitates and I mentally review the things I need to do in cases of student ethical misconduct. If he is the first to come forward with the admission, then everything will be much better for him. I think. What he says next is a complete surprise to me. "I think I'm in love with you."

In books, authors often say that a character is speechless, but in real life surely this is much rarer than one thinks. But I am speechless for a long time. Here sits this kid I have been feeling guilty about. I have got over a funny little bump in my life because I was thinking about him in a way unbecoming to someone in my position. And now here he is, opening it all up again.

Except it doesn't feel like it is opened up at all. I examine my feelings as carefully as I can. I feel like a professor with a sad student. That's all, mostly. What a relief. But we'll see what happens in my dreams tonight.

"Luke. I never thought..." He is looking me in the eyes now, with disconcerting frankness. "Thank you. Really. Thank you. Your...affection is a gift, and I...prize it." Lame. I cringe inwardly, but stumble on. I'm the adult here. I have to do something, fake some wisdom and perception. "But you...you can't stay in this space. This – this – space. We can't stay here. This is too rough on you, and, well, we just can't be here. Right?"

He nods, and says, "But there's something else. I did something stupid, in History, and I immediately regretted it. I plagiarized a paper." I say nothing, just nod, and wait. "I've been trying to figure out why. I can't fully explain it. It's so humiliating. I did it really obviously so that Connors would spot it right away, and...and punish me. Well, I guess I do know why I did it in *his* class. I know he's a friend of yours, and he would probably tell you, and this would make a splash."

This is surely counterintuitive. If I were him, I would have tried to get attention directly from the person I admired. But the heart is a funny thing. It veers and shivers and slips and blunders.

I think for a moment. This is, maybe, more complicated than I thought. I look at the kid's face. I think he really does feel something for me. There is a flush in the skin now, and something intense in the eyes. I look down. It will pass. But I think he wasn't just trying to get attention. This is a kid with a real sense of right and wrong. I've always known this about him. He is trying to get kicked out, to remove himself from my proximity.

And it suddenly seems to me he is doing this because he has interpreted something in my own behaviour that showed I was susceptible. He isn't only removing himself. He is separating us.

I say none of this. I am, surely, flushed myself by now. He is a perceptive enough person that perhaps some of his thoughts have kept pace with mine. I do not know. And I cannot know. We cannot voice this.

I pick my words carefully. "You're trying to get kicked out of university." I look for affirmation. After a moment, I get it. The coffee shop feels warm. I want to thank him again for caring about me enough to come up with this idiotic, tortuous plan that could ruin a promising academic career. His, not mine. I don't give a damn about mine. But, of course, I say nothing of the sort. "Luke." He keeps staring down at the table. I look at his hand. It is a well-formed hand, a very young hand. I will never hold this hand, and the thought makes me sad.

I'm human. I'm fallible. I have the handsomest, sexiest husband in the world, and I am sorry that I can't reach out and touch this beautiful young man. I realize I need to speak, but I don't know what to say. I had no idea this was going to happen when I left home this morning. I wish I wasn't flattered by this, but I am.

"Okay. Let's think about this History paper. I think I should stay out of this. Tom hasn't said anything to you yet, right?" Luke confirms this. "You go to him, tell him you've screwed up. You admit you've done something wrong. You take a zero on the paper. It wasn't worth a whole lot, was it, this early in term? And we'll see what Tom says. If you are the one to bring up the problem, it looks good. If I need to talk to Tom, I will, and I'll be your advocate and ask if you can stay in the course and have another chance. But it's probably best if I don't get involved. Let's keep this as simple as we can."

Outside the coffee shop, we shake hands rather formally and move in opposite directions. I know that later today he will go and do the paperwork to drop the one course of mine that he is currently enrolled in. He didn't say so, but I know he will do this. I'm the one who will have to sign the form, and I'll tell him it's a good idea, and I'll also say that I will be sorry not to have his excellent contributions in class. And that will be it. We'll stay away from each other, and he'll go to grad school, after I write him a nice recommendation.

I have no classes until two thirty, so I head back home. It is only a couple of blocks, and I need to be alone for a while. I feel like a teenager again, wanting to go to my room to lick my wounds. Didn't know it could feel this sad to be admired by someone half your age. But it does.

GOING FOR COFFEE

Jam is drunk, very drunk, and Hector has to help him out of the car. I watch from the back window, idly scratching the top of Helen's head. It is a long time since I have seen anyone this incapacitated by liquor and the sight cuts into me. Even seeing a stranger like this is hard. And this is Jam, someone I have very slowly grown to care about, at first because he belongs to Hector, and now for his own sake, the sake of his own dreadful, marvellous self. He falls in the snow beside the car and I can see him stay there, kneeling. He is laughing, I think, and Hector stands over him, speaking to him. I cannot imagine what he is saying. And Jam is still on his knees and then Hector is bending to pull him up. Hector is doing all the work, I can see, and Jam keeps laughing. I think.

I back away from the door and move towards the stairs before they can see me. I hesitate: does Hector need my help? I decide to wait in the living room and listen, to see how bad things are. I look around the room, at Hector's good black suit jacket where it shouldn't be. Under a sleeping cat. At our Modigliani prints and our tiny crystal model of the Chrysler Building in Manhattan, a two-dollar trinket we both love for no good reason. I see finally the missing CD case for the soundtrack to *Pal Joey*, in the corner where Max has thrown it. I pick it up; it is not broken. I weigh it in my hand as I listen.

"You don't *know*," says Jam, loudly, as the door swings open, bringing with it a blast of icy air. I don't know why I think, every February, that this is the month when temperatures will start to become kinder. But every year we get the coldest weather in February. "What you and Janey have. Nobody has that. Nobody has that." I hear him slip and go down just inside the door, and I hear low sounds from Hector that I can't make out. I think he is helping Jam out of his boots, while Jam discourses. The door slams. They are in. "You don't *know*." This is Jam's refrain.

The talk is unintelligible for a while, and then I hear something like "She won't let me, she won't let me." And then more mumbling and shuffling, and then Hector's voice, clearer.

"Damn it, Jam."

I move towards the back porch, ask if I can help. The sound of my voice saying this prompts in me a tiny forgotten memory of my father in a similar situation, my mother helping him out of a car. I stop the recollection. Jam does not look up at me as I enter; he is in a place – a hellish place by the looks of it – of his own imagining. Hector does look at me, with relief.

"Help me get his coat off, and I think his pants. Here. They're too full of snow. We can't track through the house. He wiped out a bunch of times."

Jam's eyes are closed now. He seems to be falling asleep. We had better move fast before he is asleep, I think. Surely he will be heavier then, harder to manipulate. "Where was he?" I ask.

"I had to go to a few places. He was at the Viscount Gort, of all places. Hardly anyone in the bar there. He was sort of talking to a VLT. I've never seen him like this." We had had a phone call from him earlier. He was laughing, and maybe crying, and making no sense, talking about "her" and then swearing. He hung up before we could figure out where he was calling from, and Hector had gone out looking.

"It's a good thing you went," I say, and we both straighten for a moment and rest, before the task of hauling Jam to his bed in the living room. I put my arms around Hector, kiss his cold cheeks and ears. I leave my lips on his cheek for a moment and feel the warmth begin underneath my touch.

"Mmmm," says Hector, and returns my embrace. Then "Okay," he says. "Lift together." And we each take a side of Jam, and drag him, mostly, to his sofa bed. I let Hector cover him up. I don't want to be Jam's mother. "He's going to feel like crap tomorrow."

"I hope he sleeps a long, long time," I say. "Let's try to get Max out of here early."

But Jam is up when I get up, drinking coffee and sitting very still at the table. I know how hard it is to sleep after drinking. Such an unnatural sleep. When I first experienced drunkenness I remember a couple of particularly haunted nights. Frightful.

"Hey, mister," I say, quietly. I am not one of those tough-love types. He looks like he needs gentle handling. I pull up beside him, and reach over to hug him. I rarely do this with Jam. I'm not a hugging person, generally, and he and I have often had a kind of prickly relationship. But if anyone ever looked in need of comfort, it is this man. Even his hair looks sick, his skin a terrible ashen colour. I notice that his hands are shaking. A bad thing for a musician, to have shaking hands. I have never noticed that he had shaking hands before.

This is new.

"Hey, Janey," he says huskily. I suspect he talked so much last night, mostly to himself, that he has nearly lost his voice.

"We were hoping you'd sleep more than this," I say. I get some coffee for myself, sit down beside him again.

"Couldn't."

I don't say anything. He is sitting there, so quietly, with his eyes closed and both his hands wrapped around the warmth of the cup. We sit in silence for at least five minutes. It feels natural, companionable. A rare thing, especially for us. I think about a meeting I have today that Beatrice will also attend. She is gunning for me, I think. Everything I do appears to pain her.

Then Jam is talking. "She won't see me, Janey. Why won't she see me? She's the – she's the only woman I ever want to – to see – ever again. And I feel like my..." His voice trails off and his eyes open. He stares, sightlessly, towards our piano. "I feel like the centre of me has fallen down to my feet, and – and – that my life is somehow leaking out of me. Damn it. Damn it."

The last time I tried to talk to Blanche about him, a couple of weeks ago, she stopped me in mid-query and held up her hand. "Not yet. Not yet." And I nodded, obedient. Now, watching my friend's spirit seep all over my dining-room floor, I wish I had pushed past her wall, her reserve. This is long enough.

IN THE EARLY EVENINGS I READ the works of Maurice Sendak and Robert Munsch. I fold laundry, hurl toys into baskets, make lists, write things on calendars, wrap kids' birthday gifts, hunt for lost plastic hamsters, surreptitiously place several tons of artwork in the recycling under the flattened cereal boxes. Hector reads the works of Eric Carle and Tomie de Paola. He goes out to get milk, glues broken parts on plastic boats, answers phone calls from Jam's music students, wires up a new light in the closet, makes a pirate hat, plunges the toilet, tries to expunge a stain on the lapel of his black jacket needed for recitals. In the late evenings I read Dickens, and Hector puts on his headphones and listens to Prokofiev.

In the first few months I knew Hector, I wrote a poem called "Prokofiev." It was something about winter, in praise of winter. I decided that Prokofiev and the Russianness of Prokofiev stood for something spectacular in the winter. I learned to make love to Hector in the winter, and there was something about the way our cold bodies grew warm in bed together that was miraculous to me. Both of our apartments were cold, and we often ended up under piles of quilts, with socks on, exploring each other's icy white bodies like we were members of the Franklin Expedition. I was listening to a lot of Prokofiev in those days. I think that at the time there was a series about him on CBC Radio, and I was listening to it as I puttered around my little bachelor suite. The lyricism and the angularity of the music suited the way I felt. The angularity was me: sharp corners, dryness, thoughts that were trying to be somehow upright. The lyricism was what Hector was bringing to me: a horizontal goodness that could let go, a singing, a youthfulness that I had thought was already over.

At the time Hector was listening to a lot of Ravel. We often listen to the same music, but at different times. Last year I was obsessed with Brahms, and

Hector with Liszt. Hector is a good player of Bach, but more often listens to the Romantics. I am more random in my choices. In the car I like to listen to The Clash, which Hector would prefer not to hear in the house. Although it is okay to listen to Radiohead in the house. But only on Saturday afternoons.

I can read Dickens anywhere – on a bus, in the bathtub, sitting up, lying in bed. I can even read Dickens when people are talking nearby, as long as what they are saying isn't too interesting. It is nearly impossible to read Henry James, for example, if there is chatter nearby. I love to read Dickens in the mild racket of the Neighbourhood Café. I am there, reading, whenever I can, lately. I drink far too many lattes. But they will, I firmly believe, get me through this winter. It is not that Dickens is light reading. Well, he is and he isn't. Reading Dickens is not unlike seeing Wagner's *Ring* cycle. Sort of.

Hector and I went to New York once and experienced a *Ring* cycle. I had never understood the power of myth before, and Dickens is sort of a mythmaker too. It was hard to explain later to people who don't know Wagner's operas what the *Ring* felt like. It felt very primeval, and it shook me right down to my roots. I can't say I enjoyed it exactly; that would be the wrong word. Nor was it beautiful, although exquisite in parts. But the whole is not about beauty. It probes the very foundations of what human beings are made up of. And not modern human beings. Human beings in their primary state, humans before civilization, in all their badness and joyousness. I wasn't even sure that I was supposed to believe that humans had primal qualities, but after the *Ring*, I couldn't argue it. There were no words to describe what I had heard anyway. It was something preverbal, something terrible and splendid and boring too. But powerful.

In Dickens, at his best, I can feel like every absurd or pathetic or appealing or grotesque or sentimental or comic character belongs to every other character. That is how I get through the sappy bits, when women are angels who are pointing upward to heaven, when stalwart rescuers tramp the roads of England for months and years looking for lost lambikins. Because in reading about one character I am somehow reading about every other character, and I've never encountered that feeling with another author. That doesn't mean that all this identification is a happy thing; I'm not sure that it is. David Copperfield does not want to be mirrored by Uriah Heep, but he is, and he knows it. The links are there.

Hector has made a music listening room beside the office, on the second floor, and I have convinced him that we can afford a chaise for me to sprawl on. This is partly because Jam has contributed some money to the household upkeep, and this unasked-for boon had "chaise" written on it, as far I was concerned. I had been haunting the fifth floor of the Bay for years, trying out various lounging things that looked good for reading. And then in the winter sales, there it was. Red velvet. A floor model a little scuffed. But really the traffic is not heavy on the Bay's fifth floor, and a little scuffing is what I like. So Hector can sit, with headphones, in a recliner, nodding and sometimes subtly conducting, and I can lounge nearby, on red velvet, in my leopard-print pyjamas, reading Dickens.

Or so I thought. The chaise is a little harder than I

imagined. And it is tricky to get the light right. I move a vintage floor lamp with a hula-girl shade back and forth behind my head. I fetch cushions to prop around me. I try putting my head at the bottom and sticking my feet up on the backrest.

"For God's sake, Janey, quit wiggling around." Hector has torn off his headphones. "Whose music room is this? If you're going to be in here you have to behave."

"I thought it was our music room. You have a studio in the basement."

"No bloody light down there."

"Anyway. You can't have two special rooms to yourself."

"You do."

"Which?"

"The office is yours."

"Oh, it is not, Hector. I might use it a little more, but that's because I'm a bloody English professor, and that's where the books are. You're a music professor, and you don't need books. You need your feelings and a couple of sticks to hit against each other."

"Crap."

"And which one is my other special room?"

Hector hesitates. He has been prattling, I think, to let off steam. "The back porch," he says.

"The back porch? Gee, thanks. I'll head down there now and sit beside the recycling box and read my novel. Stare at the boot rack."

"I insulated it and painted it for you. It's really quite attractive."

"When the sun is shining it's not bad. And when

there aren't twenty tons of Lego and Thomas the Tank Engine toys filling up every corner of the room." I have stopped wiggling now. I am lying rigidly on my chaise, my dream chaise, hating it, glaring at Hector.

And then the power goes out. It is pitch black. We wait a moment in silence but the lights don't return. We don't move. And then I hear his voice, velvety. Melodious.

"I don't suppose you want to have sex with me."

"I don't know. Not really. But I'll think about it. Give me a moment. Okay. Nothing else to do anyway."

We grope towards each other in the dark. Part of my mind is trying to recall where either matches or a flashlight might be. Nothing nearby. We try out my chaise for a while, and then Hector says, "Well, it looks great, and it's okay for the starting part, but now I think we're ready to go upstairs. To your bedroom. It's yours, you know. I painted that for you too. You just invite me into it."

"If you are satisfactory," I say, "I will consider issuing a standing invitation."

I'VE NEVER SEEN ANYONE TAKE AS LONG to recover from a hangover as Jam, this time. Or maybe he recovered quite quickly, but a kind of gloom stayed around. He speaks less and less. At work, Blanche seems chipper enough, but I suspect that she is a woman with a fairly indomitable will. She has decided to be seen as firm and secure, and that is that. Hector and I meet Tom in the faculty club to discuss the situation. Tom is growing a patchy reddish beard, the same one he tries every

January or February. They last until Easter and are painful to behold. I always look forward to Easter, when my hairless friend emerges again from the dishevelment.

We begin our report. Jam doesn't drink lately and doesn't want to go to any bar. Hector told him that he found him talking to a VLT and that shook him badly. Jam couldn't recall that, and found it a particularly humiliating detail.

"Let's give them each the gift of a holiday somewhere, a night in a B&B," says Hector. "And they'll meet by accident and fall in love all over again."

"You think everything can be solved by going to rooms that have nothing but beds in them," I say.

"Yeah. So? Okay then, Janey, why don't you invite them both out for a latté? You seem to think that a latté will solve all problems. There. Simple. Romantic difficulty solved."

Tom's thoughts are running in other directions. "What if we stir up a crisis for one of them that only the other one could solve?"

"What could that possibly be?"

"I don't know," says Tom. "A French horn crisis. He's an expert, right? And she needs to know something about the French horn desperately, for a research project, or needs to learn to play it at short notice or something. Or –" Tom is just getting warmed up. Hector and I can lean back, enjoy our drinks and let Tom work this out. "Or, he could need something translated from a language that only Blanche understands. What languages does she know?"

"English." This is Hector's helpful contribution, and he laughs at his own wit and shovels some popcorn into his mouth. "Popcorn helps with constipation," he says, looking at me. "Really. I read it in a book. And a monk said it. So it must be true."

"I feel like we're in an *Archie* comic book," I say. "We can't be matchmaking and plotting in this way. We're too old."

"What if," says Hector, "you, Janey, invite her to a concert, and Jam is playing, and she is so overcome by the beauty of it that they fall in love all over again."

"Does he have something coming up?"

"No, that's the problem. I don't think so. But – hey, what about church music? Could we get her inside a church? He's a stand-in this week at a United Church that has a great, great piano, and he could do some rocking tunes. They're into that at the United Church."

I am doubtful. "Maybe. I'm not sure about Blanche and churches. Maybe."

We say goodbye to Tom, and Hector and I head to the daycare. While we wait for the street light to change, I wrap my head in a heavy scarf and Hector stamps his feet. There are a surprising number of people on this cold corner, and I peer at them, wondering if I feel connected to all of them in some primal way.

"Hector," I say suddenly. "What about Mrs. *Dalloway?* Maybe that's our book. Do you remember the scene in *Mrs. Dalloway* where Richard Dalloway walks across the city to tell Clarissa that he loves her? You're not Rochester or Heathcliff. You're Richard Dalloway."

Even though we have not had this conversation for several months, Hector keeps pace. He needs to be reminded of the details of Woolf's novel, however. "So that's who I am? A boring Tory MP who can't tell his wife he loves her, even if he does love her, and who sleeps in a separate room? No thanks. Are those still my only choices?"

We get Max and stop at Domino's on the way home to pick up a pizza we had ordered from the phone at the faculty club, in an instance of rare organizational brilliance. When we pull up in front, Max yells, "Hooray! Cinnamon sticks!" and so we get these too, to keep the peace.

We share another beer at home, eat pizza, talk to Max about his day. It has involved photography, an experiment with water and pop bottles that somehow created a whirlpool effect and the making of bannock. Four-year-olds today have more complex and sophisticated lives than I can recall having. Age four. Hmmm. I remember having the toes of my Barbie chewed off by an older sister. I can remember helping my mother put poisonous dust on potato beetles. Not much else. Desultory activity with crayons.

"He brings her flowers. Richard Dalloway. That's something." I say this as we are unloading the dishwasher together, while Max pretends to be grooming the cats. They are both fascinated and repelled by his efforts to brush them. They rub against his legs as he sits on the kitchen floor. This tickles and he giggles. I worry that he is brushing them too hard. He seems to think sometimes that they are plush cats, game for any torment.

"Isn't Clarissa Dalloway a lesbian?" Hector eats the leftover carrot sticks from Max's plate.

"Well, yes. And no. Who knows? Does it matter? I think Clarissa and Richard really love each other. Even if she is a lesbian."

"So you're saying that I resemble the emotionally stunted conventional husband of a confused, chaste lesbian."

"Not if you put it that way. You're not entering into the spirit of the thing, Hector. Don't vex me."

"Do you have time after we put Max to bed to practise your *Griselda* songs?"

"I guess so. Let's wait until we're sure he's asleep. I suppose there aren't any couples like us in the whole world of literature. In the whole world. We are *sui generis*."

"Ah, honey, that's hubris. Don't tempt the gods to exercise their wrath upon us."

There's that word: *hubris*. First *Crystal Palace,* now *hubris*. I try to remember what else I wrote in my stream-of-consciousness diary last summer. Will all these phrases erupt into the actuality of my life? I think another one of them was something about the way my first Bible smelled. The likelihood that I will have a moment of synchronicity over this one is, I think and hope, slim.

I don't want Hector to be like Richard Dalloway. Who is, admittedly, kind of a stick. But I am still fond of the notion of Hector as Rochester, in a way. I like the idea that Rochester was willing to be a bigamist with Jane. It was shocking in 1847. Sounds sexy to me now. But I can see Hector's objections. Rochester is a crumbled edifice at the end. He has been tamed, brought to heel. Why should Hector give in to that stereotype?

"Maybe," I say, as we turn off the kitchen light, "you are more like Gilbert Blythe."

"Who?"

"Gilbert. That's the guy Anne of Green Gables marries.

He dips her red braid in an inkwell, which is a pretty bold pickup move, I think. Sort of like when you insisted on trying out all sorts of dip recipes when we first met. Dipping, dipping. I caught on pretty fast, you know. I'm not dense."

"I'd just been to Greece the Christmas before. I was into tzatziki and hummus. It was culinary, not carnal. Not amatory but alimentary." He pauses, thinking. "It was about comestibles, not canoodling." He reaches out to touch my bum, and I squirm out of his reach.

"Oh, shut up, Hector. Where was I? You're always distracting me. Gilbert and Anne. There's a good couple."

"Why? Because he dipped her braids? Ooh, Tristan und Isolde, look out."

"No, because – well, I can't really remember what their marriage was like. I read the books thirty years ago. But I remember they were happy. That's something. I guess if you can't remember much about the marriage, that's the literary definition of happiness. If you can remember, you're in trouble. The Bovarys. The Karenins. The Richard the Thirds."

"Sorry, Janey." Hector smirks at me.

"What are you sorry about?"

"I've got gas."

"Yikes."

"You know what? I think we're pretty memorable. If anyone's asking me," he says.

"WHAT IS IT?"

Jam is holding a paper out towards me. I take it. "Just read it, Janey. And tell me what you think."

You are the woman who lives in all my thoughts, who has possessed herself of all my energies, who has become the one guiding influence that now directs the purpose of my life.

"Did you write this?"

"Just tell me what you think of it."

"You didn't write this."

"Just tell me."

"It's very romantic. Umm, a certain sort of woman would give her eye teeth to receive this sort of message. I assume that's the kind of comment you're hunting for?"

Jam doesn't commit himself. He takes the paper back, folds it carefully.

"I'm not sure that Blanche is that woman. I would like it. But Blanche is a lot different from me. Is that also what you're digging for? Jam, where did it come from?"

"A novel, in your office. *The Woman in White*. Wilkie Collins."

"Really? I don't remember the writing being like that. But I guess you're right."

I am getting a sense of déjà vu. People borrowing chunks of romantic prose from other writers. I guess it's a Cyrano situation, in a way. Did it work for Cyrano de Bergerac? I think. Yes and no. He dies in the end. Mostly no.

"Maybe you could paraphrase the ideas in it. Make it less Victorian. She's a pretty contemporary woman, after all. Or maybe you should do it with music." I stop and wait for him to say something, but he doesn't. "What are you playing as prelude and postlude in that United Church tomorrow?"

He considers. "Some Debussy. Some Franck." I nod. "You know what I would go for? But again, I'm not Blanche. But I would go for Brahms."

Some colour comes into his face at last. "She told me once that she loves Brahms." It is the first hopeful look I've seen on his face in a while. "But why would she go to Waterford United?"

"I don't know. We can't come. Otherwise I would try to take her. We have our annual congregational meeting tomorrow, and I'm being nominated for church council. We have to be at our place. Vexation. Hey. Hey. Waterford? I think Jean Smothers is a member there. Doesn't go regularly, but...let me make a phone call, Jam. While I'm being brave."

Matchmaking is a deadly business. I've never seen it work. I've seen friendships die fiery deaths because of it. But I'm calling Jean anyway, and asking if she is going to church in the morning, and giving her a brief and cleaned-up version of The Blanche and Jam Story, and asking if she would be comfortable inviting Blanche to go with her. And making her promise to be discreet.

Not only is Jean keen on the idea, it is actually Bring a Friend Sunday at Waterford United. There is harmony in the universe. I get off the phone and say very little to Jam. But I offer him a share in my most prized leisure activity. "Let's go have a latté. We have to get Max from his play date next door, but then let's take him for a cinnamon bun, and I'll buy you a latté."

WALKING TO WORK

I dreamed of the Crystal Palace. Not the nine-teenth-century pleasure dome, but something of my own. But now that I try to write it down, I cannot see it. Maybe there is nothing to see. I turn the light off again, put my head back on the pillow, will myself towards the Crystal Palace. Cloudy, not crystalline at all. Hector has gone early to do an adjudication of some sort. I can hear Jam downstairs talking with Max, crashing bowls in the kitchen. I have a few minutes.

All I can discover is that it is not a structure, and it does not even seem to be a place. But I can touch it, and it is beautiful.

I get up. Today I have no classes, but I do have the children's literature conference, and my paper on talking animals. It's okay, not great. I'm a little worried. I listen at the top of the stairs, decide I'm not needed, have a shower, get dressed. And then descend.

"Read me *Max's Birthday*."

"And good morning to you too, honey."

"Read me *Max's Birthday*."

I turn to Jam. "Good morning, Jam."

He plays the game. "Good morning to you, dear lady. And how wast your nocturnal repast?"

"Excellent, fair sir. I am grateful to you for your kind inquiry."

Jam has a shirt and tie on. I narrow my eyes at him.

"And this, this...thing around your neck. It means... what exactly? Now I'm really worried about you. Even more than when you were vomiting all over the place."

"You remember. Job interview today. Music director at the little cathedral. I'm a shoo-in. I slept with the rector once. She was a big fan, as I recall."

I frown and jerk my head towards Max. "You think *Mr. Wonderful* isn't taking this all in and reporting it to his daycare workers?" I say this between clenched teeth.

"Reporting what to my daycare workers?"

"Good morning, Max."

"Hello, Mom."

"I would be happy to read *Max's Birthday* in five minutes. Okay?"

"Three minutes."

"Five minutes."

"Three minutes."

"Max."

He wanders off and I start to pack his lunch for the day.

"I'm having dinner with Blanche tonight." Jam is more relaxed than I've seen him in a while. "She's –" He stops and starts a couple of times. "It looks hopeful," is all he finally says. "We've had a couple of really, really good conversations. I haven't laid a hand on her."

"Impressive," I say.

"I thought so too. And I was sure to emphasize to her what a tremendously unusual move – lack of move, I guess – that was for me. I made her feel a little sorry for me." His smile is not as big as it used to be. He has laughed much less of late. He moves more slowly through the house, almost as if he is feeling his age. But he is more considerate. He listens to me more, sits looking thoughtfully at Max when he plays with his toys, is more helpful with musical problems that Hector is trying to solve.

We asked him, last month, about playing Brahms in church, with Blanche in the congregation. He wouldn't say anything but would only shake his head and smile. It was one of those odd shakes of the head, though, the ones that are supposed to be negative but have streaks of the affirmative.

I arrange to loan Jam the car for his interview, ask him to take Max to daycare this morning. I want to walk to work. It is part of my energetic new plan for self-care. Or something. It is getting warmer, and at least half of the snow is gone. Hector walks it all the time and has told me his secret paths through backyards and alleys.

I look at myself in the mirror. Brown power suit. Thrilling. Never mind. I check my bookbag for my presentation notes, check Max's backpack for requisite pirate flag, small red rock, his favourite tiny blue sports car. I sit down with Max on the couch, open the book.

I can remember the first time we read this book. It was the first book we received as a present when the baby was born. Hector would sit in this very spot and read it over and over to the baby, who was about three days old. "Lift him up, Janey, so he can see the pictures."

"He's sleeping, Hector. We should be too. He's only sleeping for seven minutes at a stretch. I'm going to go mad."

"*Max got a toy dragon for his birthday. No, said*

Max. So Ruby made the dragon run away. You aren't going to make my dragon run away, are you, wife?"

I remember opening my eyes. I was trying to teach myself to do power naps. I was sprawled in the corner not far from them. I remember that the baby looked tiny lying there, tucked close into Hector's body. In my own arms, Little Max looked gigantic to me. He had come out of my body. Nothing would ever be the same. This baby was the most significant thing in the entire universe. But if there was some space between the baby and me, I could begin to realize that he was small and fragile. A baby. Not a god. Not a demon. Just a baby. "Dragon? To what would you be referring?"

Hector read on. When he got to the back page, where the little rabbit decides he does not detest the dragon, but actually relishes it, Hector made the little board book dance. *"The dragon landed on top of Max. Again, said Max."* Hector raised his eyebrows at me. "Let's read it again," he said.

This book has always been one of Max's favourites. Does he remember, in some Wordsworthian remnant of childish perfect knowledge, the first readings of this book? Does he remember dozing on the couch and his father moving, crawling over to the space on the floor where his mother was propped on a million cushions, and his father peeling back her layers of clothing and covering her body with kisses? He was a good baby and slept for at least twenty minutes that time. I remember. I remember.

I have stopped reading in the middle, and Max has joggled me with his elbow. And then, getting no response, he tries it himself. *"Around the table."*

I look down, nod and turn the page. Max handles

the rest of the book, more or less correctly, from memory. It is not surprising. It has been read to him seven thousand times. Still, it is his first independent foray into reading, and I feel a great weight lifted. Everything will surely be easier from now on.

AT MY OFFICE, I HAVE ARRANGED TO MEET René, who is on his spring break from grade twelve. It is like him to spend the time working on homework, a project about pregnancy. When he told me, I tried not to be surprised. No one is making him do this; it is an optional assignment for some social science course. But I had mentioned once that I had written a pregnancy journal when I was having Max, and René had asked if he could read it, and maybe use it in the paper he is writing. While I wait for him, I open the notebook and read over some of it.

SEPTEMBER 8: I have begun to do crossword puzzles incessantly. These fill my time and occupy my mind better than most projects; it is busy work that is impersonal and demands only a certain attention span. I can't concentrate on any intellectual problem for long; soon I find I am contemplating the wall or a tree outside my window, and instead of thinking I am listening intently to something going on inside my body that I cannot quite translate correctly.

OCTOBER 2: This is an almost excruciatingly intimate time, a time that can be salutary for a marriage or, I think, terrible. If there are barriers between a man and a woman, even ones that might be small and bearable in ordinary life, in pregnancy and childbirth (and beyond, in those sleepless and emotional weeks and months) these barriers can destroy. I wonder how so many marriages survive this wonderful, terrible time.

OCTOBER 9: What does it mean when everyone says you look great? I have never had so many people compliment me on my appearance. Is it sincere? Do people genuinely like the look of a pregnant woman, the way I like the look of a garden this time of year, full of vegetables? I don't see much difference from my regular self, except for The Biggest Belly in the World. As for that monstrosity, I am adjusting to it better. One just needs to get used to it. Is it possible that pregnant women are praised for their appearance as a compensatory measure? Sympathetic onlookers, especially those who are parents, know how irritating and tiring certain aspects of pregnancy can be. Are the compliments our remuneration for putting some more human creatures on the map? After all, someone has to do it, this peopling.

I consider what a teenage boy will do with this journal, and consider also excising parts of it before he turns up. But when he comes I hand it to him with a crooked grin, telling him it is a little intimate, but to do what he wants with it. It is a frank document, I say. I trust him. He doesn't say much in return, but he doesn't seem embarrassed either. René is the New Man, I think. Comfortable with all sorts of things.

After René leaves, the next order of business is to get these peace march posters off my desk and up around campus. Except they aren't posters, just blank sheets. Nothing changes. I hunt around the hallways for likely looking volunteers and then abandon the search and go back to my office. Jiffy Marker fumes again. These markers are strange, fruit scented or something. I definitely smell grapefruit. I have been working for about a half-hour when I think a tiny, naked Al Gore is dancing on the edge of my desk, and realize I'd better open the window. Or get out of here. I do both. And prop the finished posters outside my door, in case Jee-Anne shows up to collect them.

It is eleven forty-five. I feel light-headed. I don't present my paper until two o'clock. I have looked over the conference program, and the titles for the morning have not looked promising, so I'm avoiding the hallways where the conference participants are twittering, jitterbugging, scampering delightedly through the proceedings. I feel even more light-headed. I'd better get a grip on myself. The unaccustomed walk from home, the exertion of it, must have been a mistake. And I've drugged myself with marker fumes. And then thinking again about pregnancy in all of its disconcerting strangeness. I barely knew who I was before the pregnancy, and then everything went haywire with breasts and belly and hormones and then I really didn't know who I was. I need some sugar and go to the cafeteria and eat two doughnuts. Better. The vision of the academics jitterbugging is, blissfully, fading. Even though it is a kidlit conference, and the place should be overflowing with delight, there will be, I know, not a morsel of delight anywhere. I wish I had not signed on for this.

I am more nervous than I realized. I haven't given a paper in a while. I decide I will have lunch in the faculty club, and have a drink, and go over my notes. A small voice in my head reminds me of a stretch in my twenties when I used to drink too much before stressful situations. I ignore it. Once in the faculty club I also order a beer for Tom, who is sitting talking to a History colleague in the corner of the room, but when I hold it out to him he shakes his head, points to his watch and heads out the door. I have to drink his beer.

I look at the program again. The session that will finish up soon is called Gender and Lunacy. There is a paper about a manga series that I've never heard of. The manga series involves both "translateral transgressions" and "persona brokering." I have no clue what that means and finish Tom's beer. I signal to Julia for another and eat my vegetarian sandwich. Maybe I should have had something with more heft to get me through this. Something greasy. I read in the program about another paper, about Sendak's *Where the Wild Things Are:* "Ego dislocation and maternal anxiety modification." And I just liked the part where the creatures rolled their terrible eyes and gnashed their terrible teeth.

I get to my feet. The clock says one fifteen. What can I do for forty-five minutes in my office? Nothing useful. I decide sipping on a small Scotch won't hurt me and go over to look at Julia's selection. I choose an expensive one with lots of peat in it, which I don't really like, so that I will be forced to sip it. I head back to my table, ponder the program some more. Ivan the medievalist is doing a paper tomorrow called "A Brechtian Performance of The York Mystery Cycle as Performed in 1966 by Children of the St. Jude's Orphanage and Directed by Samuel Beckett." Is this for real? I can't even tell any more what is real at these conferences. Everything seems parodic to me.

It is time to go.

WHEN I TRY TO EXPLAIN IT ALL to Hector later, he cannot help but laugh, but he also seems worried. He brings me a cool cloth for my forehead and pulls the curtains across our bedroom windows. It is almost five. Still pretty bright, or so it seems to me. Jam has taken Max with him to pick up Chinese food for us, preparatory to going out with Blanche at seven. Chinese food. I think of those noodle dishes and my stomach heaves. I take deep breaths.

"Did you really say that? Did you use the phrase 'self-congratulatory, masturbatory brain swill'? You didn't."

"I think I did." I hesitate. "You can ask Blanche later. But I think I also said at the beginning that I was sorry that my paper was a concrete study of actual books and that some of them might have difficulty following it."

Hector grimaces. "I wish I could believe that you didn't say that, Janey, but I rather suspect that you did."

"And that's not all. While I was reading the paper, these witty little quips would pop into my head, and I would let them fly." I fumble in the air, making scare quotes around *witty*. "And I knew, almost immediately, that they weren't witty at all. But I couldn't stop. I said that if I heard about Jacques Lacan's 'locus of the Other' one more time, I was going to lose it. I told them my Jacques Lacan joke. *How do you tell the Lacanian at the party? He's the one who makes you the offer you can't understand.* And then I laughed. No one else was laughing. It was gruesome and tasteless, that's what it was. And career destroying." I moan.

Hector goes off to fetch me another cup of coffee.

"Well," he says finally, after we have sat in silence for a moment. "There's still your singing career. That's good."

He lets me sleep for an hour and then comes back in with Max. "Let's watch *Robin Hood,* Mom," says Max, and he pats my arms gently, one after the other. Hector has told him I have the flu, which is very kind of him. "It will make you feel better."

I kiss the boy and swing my legs carefully off the bed. "I think you're probably right. Thank you for letting me rest, guys." I stand, warily. "Is Jam gone?"

"Yeah," says Hector. "And you know, in the flurry of the volcanic eruption that was once your career, you didn't hear about his interview. It went really well. He thinks he has it. He says he can move off our couch soon."

"I like him on our couch. What will we do without him?"

Hector and Max pass the popcorn back and forth between them. They gesture with it in my direction. I shake my head.

I THINK OF AVOIDING THE UNIVERSITY the next day, cancelling all obligations, but I find myself walking to work again. The sun is radiant and even the dirty late-winter snow is beautiful. I have that absurd feeling of almost fake well-being that means I have survived a hangover. Maybe this is why great artists drink too much. The aftermath is horrid, but the aftermath of the aftermath is miraculous. For a bit.

I pick up a latté across the street from campus, a big latté, and head in, breathing deeply. I make my way down the English Department hallway without incident. I see Jean Smothers in the distance and duck into my office. But then, a moment later, I hear a knock on the door. I have closed it, which is usually the signal that I am not there, in body or in mind. I hesitate and then open it.

Jean is standing there smiling, the picture of sanity. Everyone looks sane to me today. I am deranged. I must be. I must study the rest of these people and copy their mannerisms so I can function in this society of sane people. "Janey, my dear, how are you doing?"

"I'm okay, Jean. Come in."

She closes the door behind her and perches on the wooden chair beside my desk. How can an old woman perch so well? "I thought that was a tremendous thing you did yesterday."

I close my eyes. I had rather hoped it was a bad dream. I open my eyes and try to look brave and ironic. "Tremendously stupid, you mean? Is anyone asking for my resignation yet?"

She smiles again. Her short hair is particularly spiky today, and I think I can see a streak of purple in the grey. This distracts me in a welcome way. I don't want to think about anything serious. I love Jean's hair, hold on to it with my whole being.

"No," says Jean. "Of course not. Well, yes, there is a faction here that will hold it against you. But that wasn't a faction favourably disposed to you – or me – anyway. But in my opinion, for what it's worth, I think you were wonderful."

"Oh Jean, that's terribly kind of you. It means a lot to me. But I was a maniac. I made no sense. Did I?"

"It was a little unorthodox. But it made more sense

than most of what I'd been sitting through before that point. I thought you might be worried today, so I wanted to be the first to talk to you. You listen to me, Janey. It was all right. It was just right. It was marvellous. Everything will be fine. Trust me."

She stands up, reaches out, gives me a hug. That's a new one. Then she points to my shirt. "Now spruce yourself up. You look like shit. What is that?"

I look down. Latté. She hands me her long scarf, the kind with sparkling threads running through cloth that is variegated orange and gold and pink. I wind it around my neck several times. She nods in approval.

"I liked the part," she says, "when you called Derrida an intellectual grave-robber."

Jean leaves and I feel the need to go for a walk. I have no recall of that line. Nor do I know what it means. Will it become one of those legendary pieces of nonsense to which meaning accretes, accidentally, over the eons? I go up the back staircase towards Music. Maybe I will get a glimpse of Hector, and it will be comforting. I do see him, in a classroom with his Music History class, finishing up. I pace down the hallway towards the instrument storage rooms and find myself near the room with the large harmonium. I try the door. It opens.

There she is, the large harmonium that no one ever uses. I wonder why. It is not really that large. It is a small organ, really. That's all it is. But this one is, I suppose, large for a harmonium. Or maybe it's the way it looks in this little storage room. I don't know much about harmoniums. Harmonia?

She has feminine lines, I guess, if that's the right way of describing her curves. There's nothing sharp about this instrument, but she's solid and reassuring some-how. I hear a sound behind me. I have left the door open and in comes Hector.

"Will you play her for me?"

"Her? Why is this a her?" Hector doesn't believe in anthropomorphizing musical instruments. He thinks they are above human designations. Except for banjos and piccolos. He thinks they are little above circus-clown status. He sits down, opens up the harmonium.

He plays through the melody he has been working on for Griselda's big song at the end of his little opera. Griselda, the perfect wife, has been tested by her hus-band to the limits of endurance, and she stands, principled and strong. I suppose someone might say that Chaucer's words give us a Griselda who is a brave but perverse example of submission. But in Hector's hands the song is a noble statement of autonomy. On the harmonium the song sounds odd, much more eccle-siastical than it has before, and so a little too solemn, but the instrument adds a richness to the harmonic structure that I have not heard before. He starts to sing it himself, probably knowing I don't feel much like singing today.

> *I brought you nothing else at all indeed,*
> *Than faith and nakedness and maidenhead.*
> *And here again my clothing I restore,*
> *And, too, my wedding-ring, for evermore.*
> *The rest of all your jewels, they will be*
> *Within your chamber, as I dare maintain;*
> *Naked out of my father's house, said she,*
> *I came, and naked I return again.*

Then he sings a little refrain that he has kept in Middle English: "*and naked moot I turne again.*" He repeats it, turning it around, trying it from different musical positions.

To hear a man sing this song of a woman's place in a certain kind of marriage – a woman's place at its most abject – is a fascinating experience. I have heard him sing these words before, but today, when I feel raw, it seems like a peculiar gift that he is giving me. Hector is taking everything awful about the Griselda story into his own body and making it over, making Griselda's nakedness his. But it is also still hers. And mine. So there is no difference, no Other.

He starts to play it through again, working on the changes in a different way, and this time I sing it with him. My voice sounds strange to me in this room, thinner and higher than usual. Hector knows the melody so well by this time that he can watch me and not his hands. When he comes to the end again, and I say nothing, he closes up the harmonium, strokes it and kisses me.

"I'll take you for lunch. Let's go off campus. Brave Griselda."

JAM HAS NOT OFFICIALLY MOVED OUT of our living room. He still has stuff here, but he has not come back for five nights. I have seen Blanche, but we have both been so busy with end of term marking and meetings that I have been unable to spend the time I need to work my way through her defences. To find out what's going on. I will have to wait until Hector gets an opportunity to talk to Jam. We are not certain he is staying at her place. But where else could he be?

I dream of an orange cat sleeping by my side. When I get up, the orange cat goes everywhere with me, and it gives me a kind of protected feeling, or a special status somehow. It is a remarkably simple dream, for me. Just me and this big orange cat. Sleeping together, walking together, comforting each other.

I AM STRETCHED OUT ON THE RED velvet chaise with *A Winter's Tale* on my knee, marking passages I could put on an exam for a close-reading question. Hector is marking quizzes, sighing with exasperation, occasionally reading an answer out to amuse me, but mostly working quickly and silently. We have been at it a long while. "Listen to this one," he says. "The question asks them to name three Canadian composers. I spent a week on this with them. 'Bryan Adams, Pierre Berton, René Levesque.' They weren't paying any attention at all. At least this one made a kind of weird effort. Better than the kid who wrote, 'That French guy.'"

I can feel my joints stiffening up. I look great on this chaise, I think, but I'm not sure it's good for my posture. I stop working and close my eyes. I think I will grow my hair this summer. And not worry so much about a research project. Spend more time with Max. Everyone says this is a delightful age. There must be something in it. How many times did we go to the beach with him last summer? Not very many, really. I was fussing with my electronic journal, my murder mystery, my defunct Iris Murdoch paper. Pointless, fruitless projects. And my fantasy novel, *Emoticon*. Nothing came of this either. We might as well have proper holidays.

I hear Hector's voice again and open my eyes.

"Come away, my love, my fair one, for the winter is over."

"Did you buy peaches?" I ask him. He nods, stacks up his papers on the floor beside him. Sighs and pretends to give them a little kick.

"Shall I part my hair behind? Do I dare to eat a peach?" he says, and stretches, holding out a hand to help me up. He is a considerate husband. He has noticed that the chaise is too low, and that I am struggling to get up off it.

"That's who you are," I say. "I've got it. J. Alfred Prufrock. Not Rochester. Not Heathcliff. Not Richard Dalloway. But J. Alfred Prufrock."

"Stop it right there, Janey. I categorically deny any resemblance."

We go downstairs, cut up peaches, wait for the ice cream to soften.

"You haven't said very much, Hector, about my brave stand for public drunkenness in the university. My...my *Lucky Jim* moment. How come?"

He doesn't answer right away. "I figured when you wanted to talk about it you would. But also –" here he hesitates, choosing his words carefully, "you do tend to be awfully hard on yourself, honey. I know you. I think you believe it was worse than it actually was."

"It was pretty bad. It really was."

"But you said Jean loved it."

"Jean is off her caboose. And the only other people who have been friendly to me lately are the other alcoholics in the Department."

"You're not an alcoholic."

"So why did I do it?"

"You tell me. Why did you do it?"

"I don't know. I still feel sort of sick, thinking about my lack of control." The ice cream is soft enough now, and I dig into it.

"Well, here's what I think," says Hector. "I think you got fed up. With their pomposity. With all the affectations. And you blew up. That's all. Heaven knows I've wanted to do it a million times. Anyone sensible would. You're not cut from the same cloth as them, Janey. Thank God." He takes the scoop from me, gives himself twice as much ice cream as I have given him. "Don't be so niggardly, for God's sake, woman." He pauses. "I found out something today that I need to tell you about. I've been thinking about it a bit but I think I know what to do. I've been asked to let my name stand for Department head."

I look at him. "And?"

"No. I'm not going to do it. You and I have enough going on around here."

I nod, smile. "Thanks." I sit down, eat slowly. "You remember, don't you, that I've got church council tomorrow night? And that Max has that dental appointment on Friday? That should be fun. Like a rabid rhinoceros, that kind of fun." He nods. "We're thinking of getting Jake an Easter gift. Church council is. Really, as church people we should make more of Easter. No one gives Easter gifts. And we should. What do you think he would like?"

Hector answers instantly. "I know exactly what Jake would like. The complete *Jeeves and Wooster* on DVD. He nearly peed his pants that one time. Remember?"

"Okay." I finish my dish, reach over for his. He has

too much. "I liked the sound of the harmonium, the other day. Maybe you should use it for *Patient Griselda*. It sanctifies the story somehow, makes it more understandable. But it doesn't sound too solemn. I guess it really is a small organ, isn't it? I never thought of it that way before. Harmonium sounds so different from organ. More romantic, I guess. Or something."

"I don't know anything about small organs," says Hector.

"Shut up," I say. "Stop it."

ACKNOWLEDGEMENTS

First, a thank you to the city of Winnipeg for allowing me to mess with it. The Assiniboine River and the Bay are in their proper places and many named places are real, but some locations are imagined. In particular, the university where Hector and Janey work is none of Winnipeg's universities, and I would like to stress that any conflicts or idiocies that happen at their university could not possibly occur at either of the city's universities where I have taught, the University of Winnipeg and Canadian Mennonite University. I would particularly like to assert that no Mennonites have been harmed in the creation of this novel, and further, that this really is a work of the imagination. Really.

I am grateful to the Saskatchewan Writers' Guild for a week at the Writers' Colony at St. Peter's Abbey in Muenster in the summer of 2008. I also wrote parts of this novel over several summers at Luther Village, a wonderful church camp on Dogtooth Lake near Kenora, Ontario, while other members of my family were off learning woodcraft or discussing grace. Several friends have been encouraging over the years: Cathleen Hjalmarson, Mark Morton, Melanie Cameron, Michael Van Rooy, Stephan Christianson and Reshal Stein have all been supportive. And to my students and colleagues at Canadian Mennonite University go my heartfelt thanks.

My thanks to Kathleen Wall at *Wascana Review,* where parts of chapter two have been published, and to Nik Burton at Coteau Books, for all his help. And to have an editor to thank is a brand new experience for me. I never knew until now why authors make such a fuss about their editors. David Carpenter has to be the best editor alive, and I have long admired his fiction. Likely no one will believe me that working with David's editorial advice was one of the most fun things I've ever done. But it was. Any problems that remain are of course my own fault, and he did what he could about my perverse affection for commas.

I began this book with the notion that it might be fun to write about the joys and absurdities of family life more or less as they really are. My own sons and husband may say that I have occasionally trespassed where I ought not to have been. If so, my loving apologies.

Quotation from *Dr. Spock's Baby and Child Care* by Benjamin Spock, M.D. and Michael B. Rothbenberg, M.D. reprinted with the permission of Pocket Books, a Division of Simon & Schuster, Inc. Copyright 1945, 1946, (c) 1957, 1968, 1976, 1985 Benjamin Spock, M.D.

The lines from "All in green went my love riding," copyright 1923, 1951, (c) 1991 by the Trustees for the E. E. Cummings Trust. Copyright (c) by George James Firmage, from *Complete Poems: 1904-1962* by E. E. Cummings, edited by George J. Firmage. Used by permission of Liveright Publishing Corporation.